Between Then *and* Now

LEAH OMAR

Eden Prairie, MN

Between Then and Now

© 2023 Leah Omar

Published by:

Bronzewood Books

14920 Ironwood Ct.

Eden Prairie, MN 55346

Cover Design: Bronzewood Books

Interior Design: Bronzewood Books

Edited by: Enchanted Quill Press

Paperback ISBN-13: S

eBook ISBN-13: 978-1-949357-75-2

To Dale and Tar:

The last call always comes too soon, because when you love someone, no amount of time could ever be enough.

Chapter One

Jenna

"ROBBY CALLED," CAMILLA SAYS, AND I adjust Signe on my hip as Camilla tucks her phone into her pocket and takes her from me. "He'll be here Memorial Day."

Camilla puts Signe in her stroller, then glances at me and wills me to react. I nod and feign disinterest. After I spent time with Robby a couple of summers ago, I've done a good job avoiding him, which isn't that hard, considering he lives in Chicago.

I wish I could change things. I'd go back to that night and do everything differently, but I can't do that. I'm good at compartmentalizing, so I stay distant and pretend that seeing Robby isn't a big deal. I manage to only think about him once or twice a day now, so I'm making progress.

"For how long?" I ask Camilla as we walk down Main Street toward her store. I promised to take care of Signe while she meets with a client. "Coming in for the holiday weekend, I assume?"

Camilla squints at me, studying my face and reactions. "His assignment ended in London. He's moving back."

We reach Camilla's store, which is propped between the drug and department stores along Main Street. Signe looks up at us and whines. She's in this stage where she screams if she's ever not in motion. I unbuckle her from the stroller and lift Signe into the air, and she laughs. Oh, I love this niece of mine.

Camilla fumbles for a key to open her store, and I press her further. "Is he moving back to Chicago? How long will he be in Wheaton?"

I tiptoe around the topic of Robby. I want to know how many days he'll be here and how long I'll need to avoid him. I always do everything in my power not to let people know what he meant to me or that I'm still picking up pieces of my heart after he broke it.

There's a chance I'm being overly dramatic. My family, especially my brothers, says it's a character flaw of mine. The truth is, someone can't break your heart when they didn't own a piece of it to begin with, but he wounded something in me that I still can't seem to recover from.

She opens the store, and I follow her in with Signe against my chest.

"He's taking a sabbatical from Goldman Sachs. He'll be in Wheaton the entire summer."

My breath catches in my throat. I slowly swallow and compose myself. "The summer? All of it?"

"The entire summer," Camilla repeats as she clears the paper off her desk.

She grabs a binder off a shelf and sets it down. "I know Robby's my brother, Jenna. But you're my friend and sister-in-law. What happened there?"

I clear my throat, an unnatural cough that reeks of suspicion. "Ahh, nothing."

She flips through her binder, and when she finds the page she is looking for, she puts a post-it there. "Two summers ago, when I moved here, you were inseparable.

And now, neither of you can look in the other person's direction."

"Not true." I shake my head profusely. "When I saw him in January, right after Signe was born, we spoke. We're just not as close, I guess."

Camilla looks at me. "Robby has shared very few details. I know he can be an ass sometimes, but seriously. What the hell happened?"

I hesitate. I want to talk to Camilla about how things went south between Robby and me, but it's trivial. Some people are meant to be in our lives only for a season, and that's who Robby was to me. He slightly bruised my ego, and most of my awkwardness around him was due to embarrassment. Putting oneself out there is hard, and I had a less than desirable outcome.

"Your support is so appreciated," I say. "But Robby and I realized we weren't meant to be friends."

"It still makes no sense if you ask me."

"He and I are cool. Acquaintances. I only wish him well in life." I squeeze my lips together and force myself to quit talking. The more words that come out, the less I can take back.

Camilla sighs. "If you say so."

"Well." I put Signe back in the stroller and avoid eye contact with Camilla. "Text me when your meeting is over. Signe and I are going for a stroll and will probably stop at my parents' house."

Camilla sprinkles Signe's face with kisses. "Mommy will see you soon. You'll have so much fun with Auntie Jenna." She then stares at me. "Thank you, thank you."

Robby will be here all summer. I walk down the street toward my parents' home and process all of what that means. I've done a great job avoiding him, which is challenging. It's hard because his sister married my brother; therefore, I'm tied to Robby for life. There was

Camilla and Jake's wedding, where I was forced to see him and subsequently avoid him. And then he came to town when Signe was born.

I've mapped out all the times I'll need to avoid Robby in the next eighteen years. Signe's milestone birthdays, maybe a holiday here and there when he decides to spend it in Wheaton, and then Signe's high school graduation. Of course, it's occurred to me that Jake and Camilla may have more children, and I'll need to double, or triple, the number of family events I'll have to evade Robby at.

How will I dodge him if he's here all summer? Wheaton is not a large town. And I work a few nights every week at The Pool Hall. Everyone goes there. I won't be able to avoid him. There will be family gatherings and unwanted meetings at the grocery store, bank, or on the lake. It's inevitable.

"Signe." I look down at my four-month-old niece as she kicks her feet, enjoying the uneven pavement beneath her. "Your polo shirt loving, loafer wearing, preppy man of an uncle is coming to visit."

She pumps her arms into the air, like only an uncoordinated baby can do and still look cute. Oh, to be an oblivious baby, where life is simple, and emotions don't muddy up our interactions with people. But we all grow up and are forced to navigate the intricacies of being alive.

"You'll like me better." I adjust the bonnet on her head. "I'm cool Aunt Jenna. He's boring Uncle Robby. Don't forget that."

The last time I saw Robby was in January, when Signe was born. Jake and Camilla had a bunch of family over. Of course, I wouldn't miss it. And Robby, naturally, was going to fly in from London to meet her. We said hi, and after spending two hours amongst family, I decided that the worst was over and that I wouldn't struggle in his company anymore. I can do casual, surface-level greetings.

Yes, I went home and cried that evening. Sad that I had considered him my best friend, and now we don't even talk. I used to fixate on whose fault it was, but it doesn't even matter to me anymore. I hope it'll get easier and that I won't always be affected by his voice, face, and how different he is from any of the other guys I grew up with.

"Oh, Signe." I glance down at the stroller, and she's fast asleep, her pacifier in her lap. "What am I going to do?"

Chapter Two

Robby

*M*Y EYES ARE ON FIRE. I dig my palms into them to apply pressure and help with the burning. I've been up for over twenty-four hours, and I need to say goodbye to my grandparents, then head to the cottage.

"Grandpa."

Sunny looks up from the baseball game on in the background.

"It's getting late, and I want to settle in for the night." I yawn.

"Of course, Robby." Sunny pushes up from his blue recliner. "You can come by tomorrow if you want and meet the men for coffee. Or you can sleep late. You're a grownup. You don't need your grandpa making decisions for you."

"I'll come by in the morning to see you and Grandma." I cover the yawn that tries to escape.

"We're so happy you're here for the summer," he says. "Two of our grandchildren in Wheaton. Sis and I would never have guessed it. Would we, Sis?"

We both look at her, but she's reclined in her blue chair, eyes closed and mouth open.

I grab our ice cream bowls and bring them to the sink to rinse them. Then I give Grandpa Sunny one last hug. "I'm so happy to be here with you both. You have no idea."

"See you tomorrow, Robby." Sunny shuffles to the door and stays there to watch me leave.

The sun is low, and if I hurry to the cottage, I may be able to catch the sunset over the South Dakota horizon. I dream of that sunset, because it's one of the many things that anchors me to this place. The people that I love are here, but all the other things are part of what keeps me coming back.

I left London yesterday. I had a direct flight to Chicago, where I stopped home for a few hours to drop off my work attire and repack for a summer spent in Wheaton. And then I drove the nine hours to Wheaton.

I'm delirious from exhaustion as I drive out to the cottage on the lake with suitcases in the backseat. My bags are full of shorts, shirts, joggers, and every other piece of clothing I own that I could never wear in corporate America. It feels good to leave all my tailored suits behind. Everything about them feels stuffy and restrictive. Those suits were my uniform, and the thought of putting one on again makes my skin crawl.

This is the first time I'm unemployed since getting a campus job at eighteen. I've never been happier. I have a job waiting for me at Goldman Sachs in Chicago starting in September if I want it. It's a reward for volunteering to go to their London office for a grueling project over the past year and a half, where I spent more time in a high-rise than exploring the city.

The thing is, I'm not sure if I want to go back to Goldman Sachs. The money and security have been great, but I'm going to be thirty in a little over six months and

I'm re-evaluating everything. For my entire grown-up life, I've been happy but haven't experienced true joy. I've spent so much time climbing the corporate ladder, and now I'm at the top of it, and I'm not sure this is where I want to be.

Working my way up has afforded me money to travel and do almost anything I want, but working eighty-hour weeks gives me no free time. Most days, I'd roll into the office by seven and wouldn't leave until ten o'clock at night. The weekends had me catching up on emails I couldn't get to during the week.

Yes, I can afford a penthouse in an amazing neighborhood in Chicago, but one I can barely even enjoy.

I pull into the cottage's driveway as Camilla walks outside. I step out of my car, and she runs to me with her arms extended when she sees my car. "Robby, you're here."

She wraps her arm around my waist, and I smile into her curls. "You're a sight for sore eyes, Cam."

Motherhood suits her. She glows, and my heart swells at how happy my baby sister is. She is settled here with her husband, Jake, her baby daughter, grandparents, and a community that loves and supports her. For Camilla, Wheaton was home. For me, it's a pace of life that will allow me to gain a clearer perspective on where I want my life to go next.

"So are you." She opens the car door, grabs one of my suitcases, and wheels it through the grass. "Literally, all Sunny and the men have been talking about at the café is your coming home."

"Where's my niece?" I say as we get inside.

"Sleeping, hopefully. I left her with Jake." Camilla opens the fridge. "I stocked you up on essentials to get you through the first few days. I'm sure you're exhausted."

She then puts her hand on the coffee pot. "And you have enough coffee to get you through the summer. I splurged and got you an espresso maker." I see the shiny new contraption next to the coffee pot.

"You're a lifesaver. Truly." I peek into one of the cottage's bedrooms and decide this is where I'll stay. It has the best view of the lake.

Camilla reaches up on her tippy toes and cups my cheeks. I'm fourteen inches taller than her, and we couldn't look less like siblings if we tried. "Robby, the golden boy and favorite child, is here."

I bark a laugh. "Once you produce grandchildren, I think your status goes up significantly, so you're winning the favorite child race."

Camilla puts her hand up to her face. "You have a point."

"See." I shrug my shoulders. "I fear I've fallen out of favor. I'm now the second favorite of only two kids."

Camilla stands flat on her feet again and looks at me. "You look like crap. Like you haven't slept for days."

At the mention of sleep, I yawn. "Thanks, Cam. You've always managed to keep me humble."

Camilla laughs. "Sorry, bro, but you look really tired."

"Tired doesn't even begin to cover it."

"How long have you been up?" she asks.

I glance at my watch. "Approximately one and a half years."

Or that's what it feels like. From the moment I told my boss yes to London, I haven't slowed down. This summer, I need a different pace of life, more than I've ever needed anything in my entire life.

Camilla walks to the door, and before she has a chance to leave, I say, "Hey, Cam?"

She turns to me. "What's up?"

I hesitate and consider whether to ask because there is no way to do it without seeming like I care. The last thing I need is for Camilla, or anyone for that matter, to know how much I care. But then I ask anyway.

"When I was here in January, I overhead some talk from Dax that Jenna was looking to move out of Wheaton."

Camilla folds her arms over her chest. "And?"

"And?" I lean against the frame of the bedroom opening. "Did she move?"

Camilla relaxes her arms. "Jenna's still here. She had something in the works, but it fell through."

Shit. I'm relieved that she's here, but nervous about this little fact. Wheaton is not a big place. There will be no avoiding her this summer.

"Robby," Camilla shuts the door and walks back inside. She places her palms on the kitchen table and spreads her fingers against the grainy wood of the fifty-year-old table. "What the hell happened?"

"Cam—" I begin to say, but she cuts me off.

"You've told me so little."

I run my fingers through my hair and remember the night it all changed.

Camilla puts her hands on her hips. "Look. I've given you your privacy and stayed out of it with you and Jenna. You were literally inseparable two summers ago, and now you turn all red and stammer anytime her name is brought up."

Two summers ago was one of the best times of my entire life. I had come to Wheaton a few times to see my grandparents, and check in on Camilla, who spent the summer in Wheaton and was going through some things. Much of the summer was great until it wasn't.

"Honestly, Cam, I'm not even sure where it went south."

Another yawn escapes me. I know why things went south, but I've never understood why they're irrevocably broken. I've tried fixing things so many times, but there is only so much one can do when someone doesn't answer calls or texts. Jenna decided at some point that she didn't want me in her life, and I've done my best to respect her wishes.

"You need to fix it," she says. "We're all family. And I want Signe to be around everyone who loves her without tension. Can you do that?"

"I can try." What I don't tell Camilla is that I have tried . . . a lot.

Chapter Three

Jenna

Two Summers Ago

EYES STARED INTO ME AS I served drinks behind the outdoor bar at the Wheaton Days Street Dance. I'd started bartending at The Pool Hall to supplement my measly salary as a journalist for *Wheaton Happenings*. When I glanced up, I saw a man talking to Camilla, and we made eye contact. My skin broke into goosebumps.

He didn't remotely fit in. Everything about him screamed out of towner. He towered over Camilla, which wasn't unusual. Most people towered over her. I pressed my lips together and watched Camilla grab his arm and pull him in my direction.

I reached for two plastic cups and poured them a beer, never taking my eyes off him. "Who's your friend, Camilla?"

"This is Robby, my brother. Has he changed that much?"

Robby. Of course. I thought about how long it had been since I'd seen him. We were teenagers. He'd gotten so tall, and he grew into a man. I studied his dark brown eyes. He looked like Camilla's opposite. She's blonde with light eyes, but his hair is black, and his eyes dark. Freckles sprinkled his arms. I realized that I was staring, and I put my hand out to shake his.

"It's been a while. It's great to see you, Robby. I'm Jenna."

"You too, Jenna. It looks like we've both grown up a bit."

He gave me a flirtatious wink, and my body grew instantly warm. His voice was so low, much lower than I remember, and his words sounded like melting honey. I didn't believe in love at first sight, nor was this the first time I had seen Robby. But I did believe there were people who I had instant chemistry with. And that's how I felt when his dark eyes looked into mine. He seemed like a stranger and someone I've known my entire life, all at once.

I let go of Robby's hand, and he smiled at me and then leaned over the bar. "Will you get any free time tonight?"

"I'm off in two hours," I said, and handed them their drinks. "In the meantime, I'll keep the beers flowing."

Robby and Camilla walked away, and he looked back at me over his shoulder and smiled—that smile. I didn't recognize myself or the lump in my throat from his presence. I grew up playing with Robby and Camilla every summer, and I didn't remember ever having this sort of reaction to him.

Growing up here, attending college in a neighboring state, and not traveling much, I'd gotten used to a certain type of guy. The kind who hunted, fished, wore a camouflage sweatshirt during a night on the town and thought it's dressing up because it's clean. I was accustomed to men with sandpaper hands who were rough around the edges, even with their endearing qualities. My brothers Jake and Dax were perfect examples of the men that Wheaton produces.

But Robby, well, he was different. He looked like he was plucked from another world and transported to middle America, where he wouldn't even attempt to fit in. His polo was so pink that maybe it's not pink at all but magenta. And his dark jeans were so flawless they looked dry-cleaned. And a man like Robby wouldn't wear boot-cut jeans. No. His stopped at the ankle, which showed off the brown loafers and sockless ankles he paired with the ensemble.

The next couple of hours went by fast. My ears rang from being so close to the band, and the line never let up as people waited for their next drink. My backup tapped in, and I was off for the night.

Robby walked toward me, as if he watched me and knew when I was free.

"Hey Jenna," he said. "I was coming to find you. Camilla ran off, and my grandpa left hours ago. As it turns out, I don't know anyone else in Wheaton." He smiled as he dragged his hand across his face. It was a casual gesture, but I was completely drawn to him.

"There aren't that many people here to know."

Robby leaned into me. The band was so loud it was hard to hear anything. "Do you want to get out of here? My ears are ringing."

I held my finger to him, reached behind the bar, and grabbed two beer bottles. "Come with me. I have an idea."

Robby followed me, and we walked toward the water tower park a few blocks away. I'm not a short woman, but I still needed to strain my neck to look at him. "Are you scared of heights?"

He looked down at me. "It depends? How high are we talking?"

"High."

"Well." He put his hand up to his chin to think. "I live on the thirty-third floor of my building in Chicago. I can do some heights."

Robby put his hands on his hips. I turned my head to the side as we studied each other. "But are you like Richard Gere in Pretty Woman, where you always stay on the top floor but don't go out on the balcony?"

He barked a laugh. "I go out on my balcony."

"Great." I handed Robby a beer and took his other hand. "Follow me."

I pulled open the door to the water tower and looked back at Robby. He hesitated but didn't say anything. I turned my phone's flashlight on and walked up the spiral stairs inside the water tower.

"Do you trust me?" I asked Robby, who still stood there.

"Maybe," he answered slowly. "This might be our first real test. I'll let you know at the end of the evening."

We walked up the metal stairs that wound around the tower until we reached the top, where there was a platform. I pushed the door open, and the world beneath us opened. The music played, although it was faint from here. Robby hesitated again, but then followed me. There was a railing around the water tower, which made me feel safe. And it wasn't my first time coming up here. I sat and let my feet dangle beneath me. I patted the concrete, and Robby took a seat.

"Isn't this view beautiful?" I opened my beer.

Robby pressed his lips together. "I told you I live on the thirty-third floor and go on my balcony. But I don't dangle my feet like this."

"Relax." I nudged him on the shoulder. "I come up here a lot. This railing is steady, I promise."

Robby let out a breath and then opened his beer.

"Everyone looks like ants below us." He looked up at the sky. "And I feel like I could reach and touch the stars."

He smelled good, but not in an obnoxious way—not like he emptied a bottle of cologne all over himself sort of way. But like he just stepped out of the shower and always used dryer sheets when doing laundry. The kind of smell that told me he cared about hygiene but not vanity.

"Fill me in on the last fifteen or so years of your life." My eyes met his.

He chuckled and took another sip of his beer. "There's so much, Jenna. Where do I start? Let's see. I put down roots in Chicago after my dad retired from the foreign service. Then, I went to the University of Pennsylvania—specifically, the Wharton School of Business. I stayed there a while to get my master's degree. And then I moved back to Chicago when I got a job as an investment banker at Goldman Sachs."

I squinted and studied Robby, and he stared back at me. "What?" He asked.

How can one person say so much but give away so little? "All you did was talk about your education and where you work."

"That's a big part of my life." Robby looked away from me and put his arms on the railing. "Your turn. Tell me about yourself."

"I went to North Dakota State University on a volleyball scholarship. My high school boyfriend followed me, and we got engaged during our first year of college. We stayed together all four years, so I didn't really experience college life. We got an apartment after graduation, and I broke off the engagement. People say we should have no regrets, but dating someone throughout college is definitely a regret."

"Wait." Robby looked at me, and his mouth hung open. "That's a lot. Why'd you end things?"

"Because who I was at seventeen, and who I was at twenty-two, was no longer in line with who he was at twenty-two."

Robby nodded.

"His family still lives in town, and they hate me. They think I ruined his life, but I think I did everyone a favor. Our lives were going to be predictable. We'd move back to Wheaton, have children, and never do anything else. Someday, he will find his person and thank me for breaking things off because he'll be with the one he was always supposed to be with."

"Plus," I continued, "No one should find their person in high school."

Robby nudged me on the shoulder. "Why?"

"Think of all the college sex with strangers one would miss out on." I smirked, only partially teasing.

Robby laughed. I like that he thinks I'm funny. I also like that he put his entire body into it when he laughed. His eyes smiled, and his chest heaved.

"And now what do you want? What's next?"

"Something different, I hope." My eyes caught two people down below dancing behind where the band was playing.

"Look." I pointed. "Jake and Camilla are dancing."

"Wait, what?" Robby turned his head sharply to look down. "Together?"

"Together." I grasped Robby's chin, so he looked in the right direction.

"Why?" Robby shook his head.

"Protective big brother, are you?" I grinned.

"A little bit, yes. And Jake is, like, a lot older than my baby sister."

A sprinkle of rain landed on my nose. "Your sister is

not a baby, and I'm telling you, these two are into each other. It's a love-hate sort of relationship, but I don't know, Robby, I see some potential."

A crack of thunder roared overhead, and then it started downpouring. Robby and I shot up and darted for the door of the water tower. Once inside, we both burst out laughing and our wet clothes hung on us.

"I'm soaked," Robby said and wrung out water from his shirt.

"Follow me," I said and led him down the stairs.

When we left the water tower, the downpour had turned into sprinkles, and the band started warming up again. I went back to the outdoor bar, nodded at the bartender, and grabbed a few drinks. Then Robby and I headed back to the water tower park and sat in the glass gazebo.

We clinked our glass bottles together, and our knees touched as we sat on chairs facing each other. "Tell me something non-work related, Robby."

He looked up in thought, eyebrows knitted together. "Hmm. Well, I like Chicago. It's nice having my parents near, and I have a great group of friends. And this is kind of work-related, but being an investment banker has its perks. It's not the worst job.

"Nope, that was work-related." I poked his arm. "Try again."

Robby pushed my shoulder but smiled. "Okay. I was going to say that even though it's great money, I don't love the work. The problem is, I don't know what I want to do when I grow up."

"That's so sad, Robby." I rested my chin on my fist. "When I was little, I always knew I wanted to grow up, stay in Wheaton, and write for *Wheaton Happenings.*"

"Seriously?" Robby raised one eyebrow.

"No." I laugh again. Robby made me feel light. "That is not my dream."

He let out a sigh of relief. "Not going to lie. I'm so happy that wasn't your dream, Jenna. It's a fine dream, but I hoped yours would be different."

"By the time I'm thirty, I want to live in a large city and disappear among the masses. I want to go to graduate school for journalism. And when I'm not studying, I'll spend my time sitting on a park bench, eating some sort of pastry, and people-watching."

I continued. "Then obviously become a world-renowned journalist and all of that."

Robby leaned back on his elbows. "I love that dream for you. How old are you now?"

"Just turned twenty-six." I said, and our knees continued to press into each other.

"I'm going to hold you accountable, Jenna Abram. No slacking." Robby grinned. He smiled so easily.

"How old are you, Robby?"

"Twenty-seven," he continued. "And a half."

"By the time you're thirty, I will ensure you have a path out of investment banking."

He nodded but looked contemplative, like maybe his path to something better wasn't as attainable as mine.

Robby sat up, and I followed. He stuck his hand out for me to shake. I put my hand in his enormous hands. They were smooth, like city boy who works in an ivory tower. My heart tried to beat out of my chest, so I put my other hand on it to keep it in. I hadn't liked someone in a long time, but I was at risk of developing a huge crush on this gorgeous man who plopped into my orbit.

"Accountability partners. I like it," Robby said, holding my hand for more seconds than necessary. "Be warned, though, you'll hear from me more than you want. I'm big on accountability."

"Be warned yourself," I said as I leaned in. "I'm also big on accountability."

We stayed in that gazebo for another two hours and hardly left a topic untouched. Robby told me about his love of basketball, mainly the Chicago Bulls. We also discussed who's better, The Beatles or The Rolling Stones. Birth order. He was the oldest of two, and I was the youngest of three. We discussed Buddhism, and bucket list travel destinations, even though it seemed like Robby had already been everywhere in the world.

I told Robby why I think his sister Camilla, and my brother, Jake, were end-game material for each other. Robby made many throwing-up noises during that part of our conversation, but he promised to be open to it. I also told him how much I wished Dax would consider putting himself out there after his wife, my sister-in-law, Zari, passed away.

We finally got up from our chairs after neither of us could stop yawning. We walked toward where he was staying, and I leaned my head on his shoulder like we'd been best friends forever, and this was the most normal thing.

"You're way cooler now than you were as a kid." I smiled and wrapped my arm around his to balance myself.

Robby laughed. "Those were some of the best summers. But us boys hung out, and you and Camilla hung out. I never feel like I got to know you."

"True," I said. "You were all gross boys."

"And you and Camilla were spoiled brats." Robby winked at me.

"Also, true."

We reached his grandparents' home, and I wished we hadn't gotten there so quickly. I could talk to Robby all night. He was the easiest person I'd conversed with in a long time, maybe ever.

"This is you." I hid my disappointment.

"Who's going to walk you home?" he asked, looking down the empty street that is littered with plastic cups, bottles, and wrappers. The town had long left, so we're the last two people standing.

"You're the out-of-towner," I said. "I know where I'm going."

"Nope." Robby took my arm. "I'm also the man. I'm walking you home."

"How chivalrous." I'm not old-fashioned, but I didn't object because I'd wanted to extend my time with him in any way I could.

Robby and I walked down Main Street toward my parents' home where I was living, and we found a few more things to discuss. There was familiarity with Robby. I knew he'd head back to his life in Chicago in a couple of days, but I couldn't help but hope he'd be a big part of my life.

Chapter Four

Robby

"PLEASE COME," DAX SAYS AS we sit in the backyard of my grandparents' house having a cold drink. "Everyone will be there."

I've managed to avoid Jenna for five days. Besides going to the café with Grandpa Sunny and the grocery store during the early mornings, I've hung out at the cottage or with my grandparents. I've turned down every opportunity to be out and about, but I know I can't do this all summer, even if the rest has felt like the most needed thing in this world.

"The party is for Jenna's birthday." I fidget in my lawn chair. "She won't want me there. Trust me on this one, Dax."

Dax glances at his phone. "I already told Jenna I would invite you, and she was fine."

I raise an eyebrow. "Fine with it, was she?"

Dax nods. "We all need to move forward. Look, Robby, your sister is married to our brother. You're one of my best friends. I refuse to be one of those families who can't be in the same room together. I hate those families."

"I don't love this either. I can try to improve things with Jenna, but it's her birthday, man. She should be able to enjoy it without seeing my face."

"She doesn't dislike you as much as you think she does. That's just some narrative you've created in your head."

He may be right. There's a possibility Jenna doesn't care about me enough to dislike me at all.

Dax tucks his phone into his pocket. "She doesn't care. Come anytime on Saturday after three. Carrie and I are hosting the party at my place."

I crack my knuckles. "What should I bring?"

"Bring your swim trunks. We'll have plenty of food and beverages. That's it." Dax stands to leave. "If you're still adamant that you and Jenna need to avoid each other, there will be plenty of other people to converse with."

"You got it."

After Dax walks out, I go inside to check on Sunny and Sis. We have a meeting with the assisted living director today because our family wants to look at the potential of moving them to a place that would be easier for them. It'll be sad when we sell this house, but it's becoming less tenable for them to live here. It's a two-story building, and they can't go upstairs anymore, so their main floor office has been converted into a bedroom.

SATURDAY ARRIVES. JENNA'S BIRTHDAY. I go back and forth a hundred times on whether I should show up at Dax's. Camilla and Jake will be there with baby Signe, and Dax is right that we need to find a way to all be in a room together. We've done it before, and we can do it again. But this event feels different because it's for Jenna. I pull out of the driveway at the cottage to drive the short distance to Dax's place.

The party has already started, and I park near the cornfield as all other places are taken. People are littered across the lawn, playing volleyball and drinking. I don't see Jenna anywhere. I beeline toward Camilla, who stands by the house, holding Signe.

"Your favorite uncle is here." I take Signe and kiss her chubby cheeks. Her hair is light, like Camilla's. She grabs onto my shirt as I hold her close.

"How's my baby girl? Hello. Aren't you the cutest little girl in the entire world? Yes, you are." Camilla laughs at my baby voice.

"Good, you came." Camilla adjusts the bonnet on Signe's head.

"Yeah. Dax twisted my arm, but I probably won't stay for long." I continue to look around, and anxiety rumbles through my stomach and settles into my chest.

Camilla reaches out and grabs Signe's toe. "I just fed her, so if you want to give your sister a break for a while, she's all yours."

I pull Signe closer, and she starts babbling into my neck. "Perfect, she can be my security blanket."

"Keep her out of the sun." Camilla waves to someone and walks off. "I'll be around."

"Where should we go next?" I ask Signe, and she coos, and I give her another kiss. I never thought I could love someone as much as I love this baby girl.

Inside, a few people stand around the kitchen island, and I open the fridge to grab myself a drink. I turn around, and my breath catches. There's Jenna. Signe sees her, too, and starts kicking her feet with excitement.

It's only been a few months since I've seen her, but she still takes my breath away. Her long hair is pulled up on the top of her head, and she wears a dress over a swimsuit. Jenna's beauty is the obvious kind. Her skin is tan, her long legs are lean, and her eyes are pale blue.

It's probably not fair to other women, and it's definitely unfair to men. She has a way of putting a spell on us. Jenna Abram is somehow beautiful and the best conversationalist that ever existed.

Jenna hesitates when our eyes meet but then walks over to me. "Hey."

"Happy birthday." I smile.

Jenna looks at me like she used to, and my heart aches. I wish I could go back two years and change how things went. I'd say the things I was too scared to say back then. The words that now play on repeat in my head. If she understood how I felt, or how I still feel, I think she and I could be a part of each other's lives in some capacity.

"Thanks." Jenna reaches her arms out to Signe. "Can I?"

"She's your niece too." I hand our baby niece to Jenna.

She whispers in Signe's ear loud enough for me to hear. "What did I tell you about your preppy, loafer-loving uncle?"

Signe coos like she just heard the funniest thing.

Jenna glances up at me, and a laugh escapes my throat. I take Signe's little hand in mine.

"Is Auntie Jenna telling you lies?"

Jenna eyes my outfit. I left my swim trunks back at the cottage, not thinking I'd stay long.

"Not lies." Jenna puts Signe on her hip and points. "You're wearing orange shorts."

"Salmon," I correct her.

She then points at my shirt. "And you popped the collar on your polo."

I go to lean closer to Jenna but back away, thinking

better of it. We aren't the same people we once were. Although the banter feels like a reunion, I can't be sure yet what it means.

"To protect my neck from the sun." I look at Signe, who stares wide-eyed at me. "I wasn't blessed with the olive skin of my sister and your auntie Jenna, Signe. See the harassment I have to put up with?"

Jenna almost grins, but her lips return to a thin, straight line.

Babies are the best buffers for awkward conversations, and I continue directing my attention toward Signe, even if my words are for Jenna.

"I freckle like you wouldn't believe." I grab Signe's hand. "And no one wants a burned neck, am I right, baby girl?"

Jenna doesn't offer to give Signe back to me, so when she turns to go outside, I follow. She walks to the shade that the large maple tree provides.

She looks out at the lake, but I break this new silence. "If my calculation is correct, this is birthday twenty-eight for you."

She glances at me, seemingly surprised that I remember.

I lean against the tree. "You have two more years to get out of here and start the rest of your life."

"I'm an overachiever." Jenna sits on the hammock with Signe on her lap. "If my plan works out, I'll be gone by fall."

"Really?" I want to ask Jenna questions. What is in the works? Does she need my help? Where will she end up? But we're not at that level, I remind myself. I don't know if Jenna will ever let me back in, but if she chooses to, it will be gradual.

"Yeah." Jenna chews the inside of her lip. "I have a

few promising things in the works."

"That's not at all surprising." And it isn't—Jenna's smart. "You were never meant for this town."

Her attention turns to me. "And if my calculations are correct, you are in the last six months of your twenties."

"I have a lot to figure out between now and January."

Jenna smiles, but it doesn't reach her eyes. "A sabbatical from Goldman Sachs is probably a step in the right direction."

I want to apologize, but I've done that so many times already. I want to tell her how much I miss her and that my life has a void, not having her in it. When I tried to tell her all these things two years ago, my texts and calls went unanswered, and then her number changed. She made her point.

"Jenna," I say, unsure what to say next, so I go for realness. "I hope my being here isn't weird for you."

She stands up and hands Signe back to me. I continue. "And I don't mean just here, at your birthday party. I mean, me, here, in Wheaton. All summer."

Jenna bites her bottom lip. "Two summers ago was, well, so long ago. I can barely remember why we had a falling out in the first place. We're both older now, and looking back, maybe I overreacted. I don't know. Emotions were heightened."

Jenna is saying everything I hoped she would, yet I realize that even these words don't mean we'll return to the closeness we once had.

"I still want to be your friend, Jenna."

She presses her lips together, and her eyes look tired. I regret saying it. It's Jenna's birthday, and today isn't the day to lay all of this out for her or make things about myself. I told myself I wouldn't do this today. It's not about what I want, and I know that. It's about what Jenna wants and what makes her comfortable.

"For the past two years," Jenna says, but then pauses. "All I've wanted is to be around you and not have things feel so—"

"Weird. Awkward, and like we're both walking on eggshells?" The words come out in one long sentence.

"All the above," Jenna responds.

There is so much more I want to say, but I want to take baby steps with Jenna.

"It's incredible to see you." I adjust Signe in my arms, who starts fussing for the first time since I've been with her today.

Jenna reaches out for Signe and lets her grab her finger. "Same. I'm sure we'll see plenty of each other this summer."

Jenna sees someone behind me, and I watch her walk away. "Jenna?"

She turns.

"Happy Birthday."

Jenna nods but doesn't smile.

Chapter Five

Jenna

THERE IS RELIEF IN HAVING that first interaction over. I've been nervously looking over my shoulder all week since hearing that Robby had arrived. I hadn't seen him anywhere, which made me think that perhaps I'd heard wrong. Then there he was, at my birthday party. Dax said he would invite him, but I didn't think he would come.

I've thought of him constantly for the past couple of years, and I succeeded at keeping things surface-level the few times we were in the same room together.

Now he's here for three months, not only a night or two before he sets off somewhere new. And I hated how amazing he looked . . . and effortlessly gorgeous. I've played this out in my head several times. In my version of this story, I'd take one look at Robby and wonder why I was attracted to him in the first place.

That isn't how it happened. There he was in Dax's kitchen, holding our niece, smiling at her as she kicked her hands and legs, and it was like losing myself all over again. His voice is low. London clearly treated Robby well. Signe looked so small in his gigantic arms. And men holding babies has such an unfair pull at my heart.

I shake my head and snap any thoughts of Robby out of it. I can't go down this rabbit hole again. I read through my op-ed piece for *Wheaton Happenings* one more time. It's a small piece I wrote on Sinclair Lewis and his travels that brought him to Wheaton and the surrounding areas in the 1930s as he explored small-town living.

Then, I look over my applications for graduate programs in journalism, even before Robby reminded me that he's holding me accountable, I've been ready to move forward with the next part of my life. I submitted to five programs, none in Minnesota, and I want to, need to get into at least one of them because I need a push to leave the nest of home more than I've needed anything in my entire life. All the programs begin in January.

"Hey, Jenna," someone says and waves to me as I walk through the door of The Pool Hall for tonight's shift. I keep telling myself that the more money I save the better my chances of starting over will be. I wave back and get behind the bar to serve drinks.

It's busy, even for a Thursday. I grab a few menus and start in my section. I smile when I see Carrie and Malik sidled up to one of the high-top tables.

"Carrie, Malik." I put napkins on the faded wood surface of the table. "What brings you two in tonight?"

Carrie stands to hug me. "You didn't hear? Your parents are bringing Kylie to Fargo for her horse camp in the morning. So, Kylie is spending the night there. I thought I'd take the opportunity to enjoy a night free."

Kylie is my oldest niece, Dax's daughter with his late wife, Zari. "Oh yes, Kylie told me all about the camp. I can't believe it's already here."

It's all Kylie has talked about. I set down two menus for Carrie and Malik. "Where's Dax?"

I've always prided myself on knowing who my two brothers should end up with. No one gives me enough credit, but I'm a romantic clairvoyant. Jake ended up marrying Camilla, and Dax and Carrie are in love. I called both of those relationships from day one. Other people's lives have always been easier to navigate than mine.

"He'll be here shortly. He wanted to get Kylie settled at your parents' house first."

On cue, Dax walks through the front door and is not alone. Robby enters with him. I quickly take Carrie and Malik's orders before hurrying back to the bar. We're all friends, and more than that, we're all related to some extent now, so there will be no avoiding Robby. He and Dax have always been close.

I wait for the bartender, Gavin, to fill the drinks. I watch Dax and Robby sit next to Carrie and Malik. Then the bells on the door clink together, and I look and see Eli. My skin crawls immediately.

"Order's up," Gavin says and puts the two drinks on a tray for me.

Eli takes a seat at the bar and tries to get my attention. "Jenna, I want to talk. Five minutes. Please."

"I'm working." I wave him off. "And for the hundredth time, no."

Life is a culmination of decisions and choices. When Eli walked into my life, I was already questioning all of them. It wasn't one thing that had me feeling low, either. My life was not how I envisioned it would be at this age. And what bothered me the most was that I was doing nothing about it. My self-esteem was never lower, and sometimes I wonder if guys like Eli know that. He'll always be a reminder of what happens when I stop investing in myself and accept things, even when I'm not happy and know I can do better.

Eli isn't from here but has been a cop in a neighboring town for a decade. I dated him for nine months, which was nine months too long. In hindsight, the word dating is too strong. We hung out. He treated me poorly, but his behavior came on so gradually that before I even realized it, there I was, in an abusive relationship.

My family couldn't stand him, and they'd never had an opinion about guys I'd dated. One of the things I love most about them is that they let me live my life and make mistakes without interfering. Jake and Dax especially loathed Eli. They told me that he gave them the creeps. But I only brought him around my family a handful of times, and I never met his family.

He shows up everywhere I am and bugs me. I can't believe I let a guy like that into my life. What scares me is his delusion about our relationship. It wasn't good, it was short-lived, and so far from love.

"Here you go." I set down the drinks and turn to Dax and Robby. "What can I get you guys?"

"Hey, Jenna." Dax doesn't even bother to look at the menu. "Give me the usual, please."

"Indeed Day Tripper on tap. How about you?" I turn my attention to Robby, who looks at me briefly, but then he returns to studying the menu.

"Umm, what do you recommend?" He glances at me with his big brown eyes, and I know this is one of many interactions I'll be forced to have this summer.

I take the menu he hands to me. "We have a lot of average beer on tap. And even more average alcohol behind the bar. What are you thinking?"

"Can you make me my usual?" Robby looks at me knowingly. I hate that I know what his drink is.

"You want a Manhattan? At The Pool Hall?"

We stare at each other. "If you'll make me one, sure."

I blow out a breath, because only Robby would order this drink. "Oh, I can make you one. It will be the only

Manhattan I ever make working here."

I maneuver through the crowd to get back behind the bar. Eli still sits there, and I don't know what to do. He's a thorn in my side. My bad decision is everywhere and reminds me that I once settled for someone well below my worth. He's my reminder that my self-esteem once reached such a low level that I thought he was what I deserved. He's a dark cloud that won't leave me alone, even though I'm in a better place now.

The night goes by fast as I rush from table to table, taking orders and helping Gavin behind the bar. Carrie, Malik, Dax, and Robby stay until almost midnight. Every time I go to their table, they're laughing and seem excited to catch up. I avoid Robby's glances as much as possible because when our eyes meet, something happens inside me that time and distance didn't erase.

"You locking up?" Gavin says as he stands by the door. I still have a few tables to wipe down. His hands are on his hips, and he rubs away sweat above his eyebrow.

"I got it. I'm in again on Saturday, so I'll see you then."

Gavin leaves, and I finish cleaning up. I always like the bar to be as organized as possible for tomorrow's workers. I wipe down the tables, put the chairs up, and start mopping the floor. No matter how much I clean them, they still have the same sticky film.

The Pool Hall is my favorite place when I'm the only one here. I look around, and without all the people, I can appreciate the intricate woodwork and orderly placed table and chairs.

The bell above the door rings, and without looking up, I say, "What'd you forget, Gavin?"

"Jenna." It's all he says, but I know the voice well. My blood curls, and I tighten my grip around the mop handle.

"What do you want, Eli?" I back up, never turning

from him, until I have the bar to protect me.

"Five minutes. It's all I need."

The door opens again, and this time, Robby comes through. He left over thirty minutes ago, but here he is.

"Is everything okay?" He looks at me, then Eli, and back at me.

Eli doesn't take his eyes off me. "Things are good, man."

Robby raises an eyebrow, and I try to communicate through my look. Please don't leave me, Robby. This man is not okay. I don't trust that he won't hurt me.

"Oh, good, you're here." I lean the mop against the counter and walk toward Robby. "Thanks for picking me up."

My eyes dart to Eli. "I need to lock up for the night." I motion toward the door.

Eli hesitates but then complies. Robby stays put until Eli is out the door and stands by me as my shaky hands lock the door and pull on it to ensure I did it properly.

I can see Eli through the big window, and he walks to his car. When he gets in, I breathe a sigh of relief.

Robby squints his eyes, studying me. "Who the hell was that?"

"He's nobody." I breathe a sigh of relief for the first I've taken since Eli walked through the door.

We stand at the door momentarily. Once I know Eli is gone for good, I unlock it to leave.

"Get in." Robby opens his car door, and it's less of a request and more of a demand.

He glances at me as we drive away. "What was that about? And where am I taking you?"

"Home," I say and give directions to the house I've been renting.

"Who was that?" Robby, once again, turns in my direction before quickly looking back at the road.

I let out another big breath, not realizing how on edge I feel. "It's nothing."

Robby pulls up in front of my place, gets out, and opens my car door.

"It didn't look like nothing, Jenna. I watched him all night. There is something not right with him. My alarm bells went off."

He walks me to the door, looking around as I fumble for my key and then open the door.

I turn to him. "Why'd you come back?"

Without being asked, Robby walks in with me and looks around my place. "I walked to Sunny and Sis's to check in on them and make sure they got to bed fine. My car was parked in front of The Pool Hall, and when I came back for it, I saw him in the bar with you."

I throw my keys in a bowl on the table. I'm tired, it's late, and I decide to lay it all out there. Well, not all of it, because talking to Robby again is new. And because there is no one that I've told everything to. Because how do I explain to someone that I once chose to be with that guy?

"I dated him. Off and on. For much, much longer than I should have."

"You dated that guy?" Robby's eyebrows practically disappear into his hairline. "That guy isn't worthy of being in the same room as you."

"We didn't vibe, and I very transparently told him it wouldn't work. And now he's everywhere. He shows up at The Pool Hall when I'm working, I see him around town constantly, and he always wants to talk."

"He gives me the creeps," Robby says, pulling at the windows above my kitchen sink and then in the living room. "What if he shows up here?"

"Robby, I appreciate your concern, but there's nothing I can do." I open the fridge, grab a bottle of water, and hold it against my forehead before opening it.

"You should file a protective order against him." Robby looks down the hallway where my bedroom and bathroom are.

"If he doesn't leave me alone, maybe." I walk to the door and hold it open. "For now, I can barely keep my eyes open."

"Ugh, Jenna. I'm sorry." Robby walks to the door. "How long has he been harassing you?"

"Harassment is a strong word." I lean against the door frame. "A few months."

"Does your family know?"

"That he shows up everywhere I am?" I squeeze my eyes shut. "No. And I'd like to keep it that way."

Robby stands with his hand on the door. "Be safe."

"I will."

Robby steps outside.

"And as much as I appreciate the ride, I'm not your problem."

Robby rakes a finger across his face. "Of course, Jenna. Goodnight."

Chapter Six

Robby

Two Summer Ago

JAKE, CAMILLA, JENNA, AND I paddled toward Diamond Island. The moon and stars were the only things that lit our path. Our canoe followed the sliver of light as it sliced through the water. Jake gave me a look, and I grinned. The girls would hate us. With one dramatic lean, it tipped, and we all stood in waist-deep water. Jake and I couldn't quit laughing.

"Are you kidding me right now?" Jenna shrieked. She was not happy.

The shallow lake had a sandy bottom, and we pulled the canoe onto the shore. I glanced at Jake and Camilla who participated in a stare-off competition. Camilla was not happy. I could see it on her face. I handed Jenna a beer and grabbed her arm.

"I want to show you where just us boys hung out as kids."

Jenna and I headed to the other side of the island, which wasn't far. We walked through some shrubs and then reached the beach facing the lake's South Dakota side. Jenna's teeth chattered, and we sat on the sand, and I wrapped my arms around her.

"You're shivering." I rubbed my arms up and down her arms which were filled with goosebumps.

She looked up at me, and I was sure I'd never seen more blue eyes. Jenna was tall as a kid and all long and uncoordinated limbs. But she grew into her body nicely. If she lived in Chicago, she couldn't go to a bar without being hit on constantly. But the best thing about Jenna was that she had no idea how gorgeous she was. She was funny, down to earth, and gave off the girl next door vibe.

Jenna wrapped her arms around me. "Did you have to tip the canoe? I'm freezing. And wet. And all sandy."

"Well." I lay back because the stars were too bright and beautiful not to admire them. "You're right. Something is going on with Jake and Camilla. And I thought this would maybe help."

Jenna turned her face to me. "Wait. Your master plan was to get your sister soaking wet to hurry things between her and Jake?"

"Shit." I shook my head. "First of all. Gross. And secondly, I'm the worst wingman in the entire world. You should know this about me."

I turned to face her too. We were just two bodies, flat on our backs, and we morphed into the sand beneath us. "And what was your plan, genius?"

Jenna raised her eyebrows and then smiled. "Bringing alcohol, and Camilla having a beer, and then being unable to drive back to town."

"And?" I still wasn't understanding.

"Dax is already in a guestroom. I'll be in the other one. Jake doesn't have furniture yet, so she'll have to sleep in his room."

"You are a genius. You're much better at this stuff

than I am."

"I know." Jenna poked my chest. "And you're right. I am a genius."

"If we play our cards right." I gripped her finger. "You and I could be related."

"That's not how it works, Robby. My brother marrying your sister does not make you and I relatives."

Jenna could make a man lose himself with just one glance. I couldn't let that happen. I have an entire, full life back in Chicago. Commitments. People. No part of where I was going aligned with Jenna's path. I shook my head, trying to remove these thoughts.

"Can I ask you something, Jenna?"

Her eyes lit up, and she nodded. "But only if I can ask you something too. You first?"

I laid my hand in the space between us and pushed down in the sand. "How hard was it to break up with your high school boyfriend? I mean, after all those years, how'd you know it was the right thing to do?"

Jenna put her hand on my arm and rubbed warmth into my limbs. "I knew without a doubt. I knew. I could have spent my entire life with that guy and had a nice life. But I wanted, want, something so much more than that."

"A nice life sounds, well, nice."

"But I decided that I deserve extraordinary." Jenna put her hand in the sand and pulled up fistfuls of it. "After I did it, I felt such relief. I hate change like the next person, but the older I get, the more I am confident of what I want in my life."

"And what do you want?"

"Easy things." Jenna closed her eyes. "A man that looks up from his cell phone when I'm talking. Someone who will remove their socks before sex. A man who pauses his video game to greet me at the door when I get home from work."

"You need higher standards." I ran my hand over the stubble on my face. "Okay, your turn. What's your question?"

Her face fell flat, eyebrows cinched, and she leaned closer and lowered her voice to almost a whisper. She glanced down at my body, and then her eyes darted to mine. "I've been dying to know, Robby. Do you dry clean your jeans?"

There was no containing the laugh that came out of my mouth. It built in my chest and came barreling out.

"Yes, Jenna. I do. I only buy designer, and they're delicate."

"So pretentious." Jenna shook her head, held her hands together, and mocked me. "I only buy designer."

"Nice." I shook my head, squeezed my eyes shut, and smiled. "Now you're making fun of me."

"Designer jeans." She said it again for good measure.

We walked to the other side of the very small island, clearly interrupting something. Both Jake and Camilla jumped away from each other, and then Jenna suggested we get into the canoe to head back to Jake's home.

When we reached the shore, Jenna took my hand and pulled me inside while Camilla helped Jake put the fire out.

We went inside, Jenna poured us a drink, and then she took me into the bedroom. She put her hands behind her back and then looked at me.

"Pick a number, Robby. One or two?"

I had no idea where she was going with this question. "Umm, two."

"You win." Jenna brought her hands from behind her back and displayed her hand with two fingers held up. "Your choice. Bed or mattress on the floor?"

The room had one bed, it looked to be a queen size, with plenty of floor space. She opened the massive closet with a mattress pushed up against the wall. I should have chosen option three and gotten the hell out of this room with Jenna. Sleeping in a bedroom with her, even if on the floor, broke every one of my rules and got me further into this thing with her than I should.

"Jenna, I would never sleep in a bed if you were on the floor." I glanced again at the bed and stepped further in. "You get the bed. I'll sleep on the mattress."

I'm nervous about what would have happened without an extra mattress. I didn't trust myself around her. Everything felt too easy and natural, and I liked who I was when I was with her.

Jenna rinsed off in the shower first, and when she was done, I did the same. We laughed as we grabbed clothes from the dresser and put them on as pajamas. Jake is not a small guy. He's about six feet, five inches tall, and muscular. He used to play in the NFL. His clothes were loose on me, but on Jenna's thin frame, they were ridiculous.

She spun for me and pulled at the elastic that she rolls about three times. "On a scale of one to ten, how ridiculous do I look?"

I put sheets on the mattress, but I glanced at her as she held a fist up to her mouth like a microphone. "You're adorable." I shouldn't have said that to her, but it was true.

Jenna hopped into bed too. "Where's the best place you ever lived?"

I leaned against my arm. "Oh, for sure, Portugal. Or Chicago."

Jenna plumped her pillow. "Okay. Would you rather

be able to see ten minutes into the future or one hundred years into the future?"

"Hmm." I thought about her random question. "Neither. But one year into the future would be great."

"One year." Jenna closed her eyes, but only for a moment. "And if you had to guess where your life would be in one year, what would you say?"

I thought about that, and then I smiled. "Maybe in Chicago. Or somewhere else. You'd be my best friend, of course."

The word friend is thrown out with purpose. I've drawn a line in the sand. A necessary one that I needed her to know existed.

"Ahh, Robby." Jenna bent down to where my mattress was and gave me a fist bump. "That's the nicest thing you've ever said to me."

Jenna and I were still awake as the sun peeked through the hills on the Minnesota side and shined through the window in our room. We hadn't slept. And how could we? There was always too much to say when we're together.

She told me about some of the dreams she had. Jenna loved writing and would have loved to enter a graduate journalism program. She hadn't traveled much but wanted to. She even demonstrated her Irish River Dance, which her mom had her in for three years when she was younger. It was a weird night of safety, being heard, and light conversation.

"Jenna." I blinked rapidly, trying with everything in me to keep sleep at bay. I returned to Chicago in two days, and I didn't want to waste time sleeping.

"What's up, Robby?" Jenna held her hand in front of her face and hid a yawn.

"Do you really think Camilla and Jake are into each other?"

"One thousand percent. Yes." Jenna pulled the blanket up to her face. "Jake Abram has met his match."

Now it was my turn to yawn. "Why are you so focused on your brother? Or brothers?"

Jenna shut her eyes and smiled. "I'm happiest when the people I love are happy."

This time, Jenna's eyes didn't dart open. They stayed closed, and her mouth turned up in a smile. I reached up to the nightstand and turned the lamp off, and the dawn of a new day shone through the window. I ran through my top five happiest days ever. Days that made me feel invincible and my heart full. Today easily made it to my top five. Jenna made me feel like I was the most interesting person in any room I entered. But it wasn't me that was interesting. It was Jenna. All Jenna.

Chapter Seven

Jenna

THE SCREEN STARES BACK AT me, and I triple-check my final journalism school application and ensure I copied the correct drafts of my writing samples. Once I feel confident that I filled everything out correctly, I hit send. All five applications are out in the world, and all I can do is wait.

Being accepted into one of these programs would guarantee me a departure from Minnesota. Although, I've wanted to see something else, to live somewhere else, almost as long as I can remember, escaping Eli has become part of that desire and made the issue more urgent.

Sometimes when we're stuck, we're too far in it to recognize or to get unstuck. So many of my decisions in the past few years are questionable. Moving back to Wheaton after college graduation instead of going directly to graduate school. Robby. My entire relationship with Eli. The one decision I stand behind is breaking off my engagement to a man I no longer loved. But everything since that broken engagement has been drama. And if Eli doesn't back off, I don't know what I'll do. I feel like

I'm up against time.

We are all a myriad of decisions, and each one has the potential to lead us down a different path. My choices have me living in my hometown, which is not where I wanted to be at this stage of life. I continue to further understand the impact of every decision we make.

My feeling stuck has also affected my relationships with people in town. My best friends I had growing up never moved back to Wheaton after college, and my classmates who still live here aren't the ones I connected with much. I spend most of my free time hanging out with my family, whom I adore. But there is not that one person keeping me here.

There's a knock at the door, and my first reaction is to jump and then drop to the ground, until my head is pressed against my rug on the hardwood floors. I rent this house and have taken precautions not to have my address listed anywhere. I don't even have a mailing address and, instead, go to the post office every day for my mail. But Wheaton isn't a big town, and Eli is a cop. It wouldn't take much for him to figure out where I live.

There's a louder knock, and I army crawl to the window and push the curtain aside. Relief sweeps over me when I see my mom's car. I rush to the door.

"Mom," I say, out of breath.

"Hi, Jenna. I had some errands to run downtown and figured you'd be headed to the paper. Do you want a lift?" My mom motions toward her car.

"It's five blocks. And it's beautiful out. I can walk."

I open the door further and motion for my mom to come inside. She drops her purse on the floor and smiles. "I guess I must devise a better excuse to see my daughter."

She follows me into the kitchen, and I pour her a cup of coffee. She sits at the corner of the table in the eat-in kitchen, looks out the window, and lets out an exaggerated sigh.

"I worry about you, Jenna."

If my mom knew everything, she'd worry even more, but I hold so much back from her. I know that moms worry, and as far as my mom is concerned, she's an equal opportunity worrier, but her focus is on me these days.

It used to be Jake. When he moved back to Wheaton a few years ago, his life was a mess, and it nearly caused my mom to have a stroke. Then Jake got his life in order, started a business, and met Camilla. Then she moved on to worrying about Dax after Zari died. She was mourning the loss of her daughter-in-law and wanted to fix things for him. Now Dax is doing well, he's going to therapy, and in a serious relationship with Carrie.

Which means it's my turn. I'm now the child who doesn't have her shit together, the one the rest of the family whispers about at family gatherings. Why is Jenna underemployed? Why doesn't she own a home yet? Why is she still a bartender? The questions are endless, and the whispering is purposefully loud enough for me to hear.

I sit at the table across from her. "I know you worry, honestly, things are looking up. I feel a sense of motivation and purpose I haven't felt in years."

My mom rests the mug against her lips and closes her eyes. "If you were happy, Jenna, everything would be different. If you want to be a bartender and work at the paper, I'd be happy for you, but you're not happy."

"I'm not unhappy—"

"But," my mom interrupts. "You need to aim higher. Happy should be your target."

She's not wrong. I always saw life as linear before mine went off course. I worked hard in school to be a great student and athlete. When I graduated, my grades were good, and I played volleyball in college. In my head, I was going to become a rock-star journalist. After college, I'd do a master's program, and then move into a large city in a good market. I was going to live in a modern loft, and after I was established, meet a successful and handsome man who took the best features from Patrick Dempsey and Jamie Dornan.

Instead, I'm closer to thirty than twenty, living in a rental house in my hometown, because I was embarrassed to still live with my parents and working two part-time jobs.

"My applications are in," I tell her. "Now I wait."

My mom stands, walks to the sink, and rinses her mug. "I hope one of these schools is the answer, Jenna. You have so much potential."

I don't tell my mom that I no longer believe there is an answer. There isn't this one thing, like graduate school, that will turn my life around. The only way out of my funk is to continue. It took me many years to realize that, but now I know that moving out of this town would be the next thing, but not the answer. There are no answers, only a multitude of choices.

"It's going to work out." I walk my mom to the door and lock it behind me. I then get in her car, taking her up on the offer to drive me.

I ARRIVE AT THE OFFICE for *Wheaton Happenings*, which has recently grown to ten employees as the market has increased by five other towns, all within a sixty-mile radius. I write two weekly articles, which isn't enough money to live on, but it keeps me writing. I've also had some success submitting articles for publication in larger magazines. All of this has helped me build a decent portfolio.

"Hey there, Jenna." John, the editor-in-chief steps out of his office, which is not much more than a closet with a desk and computer. He leans against the door. "Have you decided on your next piece?"

"There are a couple of ideas I'm considering." I toss my bag on my desk and plug in my laptop. "I was thinking about a story about the new winery in Gracetown. Maybe spend a day there and write about how it got started. Something like that."

John reaches for the pen tucked behind his ear and taps it against his jeans. "That could work. But I think it would be fun to do a story on that new boy spending the summer here, taking care of his grandparents."

My heart nearly stops, and I lean forward. "Robby Bergland?"

John points his pen at me. "That's the one."

"But," I protest, "you already did that one-line write-up saying that he arrived in town."

Wheaton is notorious for announcing when people arrive. It's one of the things we're best known for.

John blows out a breath. "I want an actual article. Not a town announcement."

My goal has been to survive the summer with as few interactions as possible. Having to interview Robby for a story is not what I need right now. "I don't see it. I mean, what's the angle?"

"You can create whatever angle makes sense to you, Jenna." John waves at Pearl across the room when she arrives. "I think our readers would like a personal piece. A successful corporate businessman living in London returns to Wheaton for the summer to take care of his grandparents and assess what to do next with his life. Our readers would eat something like that up."

I stare at the blank page on my computer. The cursor blinks as if to tease me. "I could think of a few questions and email them to him, see if he's interested."

"Jenna," John says, back turned to me, heading into his closet of an office. "Set up some time with him and have it on my desk in the next few days."

There is no point in arguing. When John's mind is made up on a story, he's relentless. "You got it, boss."

John's office door slams shut, and I contemplate if I know enough about Robby's journey to Wheaton to fill in the blanks. Maybe I could write a good story without having to converse with him at all.

Chapter Eight

Robby

THE MAIN STREET CAFÉ IS bustling with energy this morning. Farmers take up a few of the tables. They've already been in the fields and are here for a morning break. They talk about everything from this year's crop—corn—how we're already behind on rainfall this summer, and the grain prices.

Sunny points at his friends, Walt, Juan, and Lawson, and we sit with them.

"Hey, gentleman," Sunny says, and I help him into the chair.

Walt moves over to make room. "No gentleman here, Sunny."

"You're looking good today, Robby." Juan hands me a cup of coffee that was already ordered. "The fresh air looks good on you."

Walt turns and swats Juan in the arm. "Last I checked, London has fresh air too."

"Not fresh." Juan swats Walt back. "More like polluted with exhaust and pretension."

"The air is definitely fresher here," I say, sipping my hot coffee. "And sleeping is easier here, too. I love opening the windows and hearing the waves with a good wind. I get why you guys love it here so much."

"Have you done any fishing yet?" Lawson asks me, adjusting his gray tracksuit.

"Not much," I admit. "I put a line off the dock the other night but caught nothing but a massive catfish."

I've never been much of an angler or outdoorsman. I wasn't the kid who played in the mud and dug up worms. I have always preferred finer things and indoor spaces. I don't tell the men that once I caught the catfish, I had no idea how to get the hook out of its mouth, so I cut the entire line.

Camping and the outdoors never made much sense to me. Why would someone sleep on the hard ground when a bed was available? If it's the view one's after, open the windows and look outside.

Juan leans forward, assessing the room before he speaks. "Don't tell anyone this, but I was at the south dam last night after dinner, pulling in walleye faster than I could get them into the live well."

"You lie," Walt and Lawson say at the same time.

Juan shakes his head, and Sunny jumps in. "What were you catching them on?"

"Crawlers. Straight crawlers."

The regular waitress, Amy, brings the men eggs and toast. It gets quiet for a moment, but then Walt looks at me. "What's the plan, son? After you leave Wheaton."

Everyone asks me this, and I never know how to answer. Chicago, in so many ways, feels like my past. My condo is there, and a job will be waiting if I want it, but I have also been exploring other options.

"We'll see, Walt," I finally answer.

Juan shakes his head. "Kids these days. Always trying to find themselves. My generation knew who we were the moment we were born."

"Oh, Juan," Walt interrupts. "You're jealous that kids have the option to find themselves these days. Your life was figured out for you."

Lawson throws his hand down on the table. "Kids act like there is some magic equation in life. Most of us die without finding ourselves. Life's a journey. Enjoy it."

The banter continues, and I sit back in my chair, listening to these four men talk about everything from the weather to fishing to a card game they recently played. Every day, it's a similar conversation. My phone vibrates in my pocket from a number I don't recognize.

"It's Jenna," the text says. "I changed my number a while ago. *Wheaton Happenings* wants to do a story on you. Are you willing?"

Before I respond, I save Jenna's new number and erase the old one. I have always kept her number in my phone, even if she hasn't answered a text from me in ages. Now I wonder how long she's had this new number.

"I'm boring, but happy to if the paper wants to do a story on me." I hold my phone and watch the three dots.

"I work tonight but am free tomorrow afternoon."

My mind goes to that man, waiting for her outside The Pool Hall, wanting to talk to her, and the fear written all over Jenna's face and body.

"What time are you off tonight?" I text her.

"Bar closes at midnight or whenever the last customer leaves."

"I'll meet you there."

"Kind of late, don't you think?"

"Not for a man without a job."

The three dots appear and disappear. I stare at my phone, waiting.

Her text finally comes through. "Okay."

WHEN I ARRIVE AT THE Pool Hall at nine-thirty, it's already empty, and Jenna washes down the tables. When the bell on the door announces my arrival, she glances at me. I walk to the bar and take a seat, and then Jenna goes to the door and locks it.

"I doubt anyone will stumble in at this time. It's been dead all night."

There's still an awkwardness with Jenna. I feel it, and I'm sure she does too. We tiptoe around each other, and neither of us is being our entire selves. Instead, we're polite but guarded.

Jenna walks around the bar and starts making me a Manhattan. I watch as she carefully measures everything and then hands me the glass. "I made it extra strong, you know, to get you to talk so I can write a truly salacious piece."

I bark a laugh, and Jenna walks around the bar and sits beside me. "You're going to be disappointed. My life is anything but salacious."

"Thanks for agreeing to do this." Jenna reaches into her bag and pulls out a notebook and a pen. "John wanted to do a story on you. Living in London, coming back to Wheaton. You know? That sort of thing."

Jenna reaches inside her bag again and pulls out a ponytail holder. She grabs a fistful of hair and ties it on top of her head. When her eyes look up again, she catches me staring at her. I hold her gaze for too long, then look away.

"Umm, yeah, sounds great. Whatever you need."

Jenna turns to me and crosses her legs. "Let's start with your education. Where'd you study, and what were you hoping to do with that degree?"

"Jenna." I lean my elbow on the counter. "You already know all of this."

She coughs. "You get to decide where this story goes. Pretend I know nothing about you. What do you want to share?"

"What do I want to share?" I raise an eyebrow.

She leans forward, looking around the bar. "If I write the story about everything I know about you, your good boy image would be ruined."

"So true." The corners of her lips turn up in a smile. "My life has been one big sensational debacle."

"Exactly." Jenna points her pen and notebook at me.

"Well, I went to Wharton and got an undergraduate degree in finance. And then, I got an MBA, also in finance also from Wharton. Damn, Jenna, I'm even boring myself. No one would want to read this stuff."

"It's fine. Go on." She waves a finger at me.

"I always wanted to be an investment banker, and after spending my childhood moving around every few years, my goal was to settle in one place for the rest of my life, which is why I landed in Chicago."

Jenna looks up at me again, this time shaking her head. "You always wanted to be an investment banker?"

"You're a relentless journalist, Jenna. Making fun of your subjects." I shake my head but laugh. There's brevity and lightness, and I can't tell if she's teasing or flirty.

"Why did you move around so much in your childhood?" She taps her pen against her notebook.

"Jenna," I say. "You know why. Do we really have to start at the beginning?"

She lets out a deep and audible breath and then pushes her lips into a line. "Fine, I'll fill in the blanks there."

"Robby," she continues, "I know it was important for you to put down roots somewhere. Did that make it hard to go to London for an assignment?"

"It did," I admit. "It was also an opportunity that wasn't really asked of me. If I wanted to continue to advance in my career, I needed to spend time at the London office."

I tell Jenna all about London. On weekends, some colleagues and I would go to Paris, Amsterdam, or Dublin for the weekend. I tell her about how London solidified my love of Indian food and got me obsessed with English football—especially the Tottenham Hotspur Football Club.

When I'm done talking, Jenna looks at me but says nothing. I take a sip of my drink. "Do I have something on my face?"

"No." Jenna shakes her head, and her face flushes with colors. "It's just, well, London sounds amazing. I've never been. Well, to be clear, I've never been to most places."

"You've been to Chicago," I remind her.

Her lips go to a flat line as she conjures a memory of Chicago.

Jenna shakes her head and moves the questions forward. "Was it hard coming to Wheaton? Especially after experiencing a place like London? Which must feel like the complete opposite."

"Honestly, no." I brush my hand against my stubble. "London was an adventure, but no one I loved was there, and I was ready to leave. Wheaton, although not my home, felt like coming home. And seeing my grandparents every day has been the best thing in the world. And my sister is here, and my baby niece. I haven't once regretted the decision."

Jenna looks at me with no expression. "What's next for you?"

The question is heavier than Jenna realizes. I've been looking into many options, and the one I'm most interested in guarantees that my salary will be desecrated, and Wharton would have been for nothing.

"I've been fortunate to have such a great career. I look forward to exploring all options, including returning to Goldman Sachs. The company has been so good to me over the years."

Jenna looks at me, furrows her brow, and feigns a yawn. "That was such a bullshit response."

I finish my drink and put the glass down. "That's what you can print."

Jenna leans in. "Okay, but now give me a real response. Pretend we're friends."

My body stiffens. Jenna went from being my best friend to someone I'm now pretending with. It amazes me how quickly a relationship can change. She glances toward the door, so I do the same. Jenna looks on edge, but I don't see anyone on the other side.

"Off the record?"

Jenna nods. "Whatever you want."

"I want to get the fuck out of investment banking."

Jenna perks up, and one side of her mouth moves to a grin. "Finally, something real is coming out of your mouth."

"I spent so much money on my education. I make a shit ton of money doing investment banking, but every day, I feel like I'm selling my soul. Literally, selling my soul."

Jenna closes her notebook, puts her pen down, and then leans back in her chair. "Did you ever like it?"

"Sure," I say. "At first. But the hours are long, and I can't enjoy anything the money affords me. I'm not even thirty years old and already burnt out.

"I made London sound all sexy for this article," I continue. "But I was there for a year and a half, and three of those weekends, I got to get away. Three. The other weekends, I was working."

Our conversation is nothing more than an interview, and I realize that, but I miss this girl. Everything about her, and I wish I hadn't lied by omission, so I could reach across to her, pull her into my chest, and hold her. Because sharing this stuff, whether she's wearing the hat of a reporter or not, is the easiest thing I've ever done.

"I hope you find what you're looking for."

Jenna stands up, and I glance at my watch. How did time pass so quickly? It's nearly midnight, and it feels like we've only been talking for a minute. That's how it always is with her. Time moves swiftly, and every time I leave her, I wish we had more of it.

"What about you, Jenna?" I put my arm on her wrist and then remove it. "What's next for you? Or are you happy here?"

Jenna bites her bottom lip and then stuffs her notebook in her bag. "I'm not qualified for anything more than writing for a small newspaper and waiting tables, right Robby?"

She looks at me, and I shake my head. "Jenna. No. You could do—"

Jenna cuts me off before I can continue. "Two summers ago, the day after." She pauses, swallows hard, and then continues. "I heard you tell Camilla that you wish I were more motivated. That I seem stuck and unmotivated."

I'm instantly cold and clammy. I know what she's referring to, but I had no idea she heard that conversation, nor does she grasp the context of what I was saying. I have only ever thought the world of Jenna.

"Jenna," I continue. "You heard everything so wrong."

"Did I, though?" She furrows her eyebrows.

"That's not what I think about you. My mind, well, it was messed up. I was frustrated by your negative self-talk, and—"

"Robby," Jenna cuts me off. "I have enough content. I appreciate your time."

She walks toward the door, and I feel defeated. Jenna is so closed off, and if she won't let me explain things, how can I ever make things right?

"Jenna." I grab her arm, and she turns to me. "For what it's worth, I think you're the most capable person I've ever met, and you're going to accomplish whatever you set your mind to."

Jenna takes a deep breath through her nose and then releases it. "Goodnight, Robby. Thanks again."

And with that, she turns away from me to lock up the bar. I stand, wait for her to get in her car, and drive away.

Chapter Nine

Jenna

THE SUN IS SO BRIGHT with the afternoon sun that even with my sunglasses and car visor, I need to hold up a hand to see. Dax called me last night to ask if I would babysit Kylie today as he and Carrie are headed to the new winery everyone is talking about. The one that John isn't interested in me covering for the newspaper.

I knock once and then push the door open. "Auntie Jenna is here." Kylie stands in the kitchen, talking to Dax, but then runs to me and slings herself into my arms.

"Auntie," she says, nestling her head into my neck. "What are we going to do today? I have so many ideas. I wrote out a list."

Carrie walks out of the bathroom, fully glammed up with her auburn hair hanging loose, and smiles. "Thanks so much for watching Kylie. You are seriously the best."

"Yes, thanks, Jenna," Dax says as he grabs the keys from the counter.

Dax opens the fridge. "Carrie made some picnic baskets. Kylie's idea. And I don't know, we'll be home in a few hours, but you know how to reach us."

"I do." I set Kylie down, and she takes my hand and walks me from the door into the kitchen.

"You kids are headed to that new winery, huh?" I ask.

"It's supposed to be great." Carrie turns to Dax. "Why is Jenna babysitting instead of coming with us?"

Dax kisses me on the cheek and walks to the door. "Because my parents weren't free."

I'm happy to be spending time with Kylie, though. One-on-one time with her is rare, and she is one of the coolest kids I've ever known. Being an aunt means I get all the love without the immense responsibility of parenting these kids.

"If you like the wine, you can thank me by bringing me a bottle or two."

"Thanks again," Carrie says, lingering in the door. "Love you so much, Kylie. See you soon."

"And guys," I say. "Take your time. Kylie and I do not need you guys rushing home."

After the longest Minnesota goodbye, where Dax and Carrie stand in the doorway reminding me of where things are, telling Kylie how much they love her, and then somehow bringing up the weather, they leave. Finally, it's just Kylie and me. I turn to her, and she's already grabbing the lunches from the fridge and putting them on the table.

I point toward the basket. "Should we go on a picnic? At Bergland Point? With drinks too. Oh, and a blanket."

Bergland Point is right between Dax's house and Jake and Camilla's. It's got a beautiful view of the lake and a nice grassy area, perfect for picnics.

"Let's grab some spicy water, and I'll get a picnic blanket from the closet."

Kylie claps her hands together, I load everything up, and we head out on our walk to the point. I hold the basket, and Kylie carries the blanket.

She looks up at me. "Carrie has been letting me help at the bed-and-breakfast. She has me remove the bedding, and I bring it to the laundry room."

"I bet you're a great helper."

We turn left at the fork in the road. "Carrie never sleeps there, though. She stays with Daddy and me. She sleeps in Daddy's room with him."

I look down at her. "Do you like that?"

Kylie giggles. "Yeah. Sometimes I get to cuddle in bed with them too. Every day, Carrie makes a yummy breakfast. It's like a sleepover every night."

We reach the point, and Kylie lays out the blanket. This beautiful child has gone through so much in her short life. She seems happy, and Dax has new life breathed into him. My brothers are happy and settled. I understand why my mom worries about me the most. Happiness is elusive because it's not a destination, and I don't always know what turn to take.

Kylie and I get situated on the blankets, and she pulls the food out of the basket. "Carrie made turkey and cheese sandwiches. With a little bit of mayonnaise because I don't like too much of that stuff."

Kylie's face lights up and sparkles when she talks about her family. I lean in and kiss her cheek. "Turkey and cheese sandwiches are my favorite."

Kylie looks at something behind me, and her brown eyes widen. She points. "Look, it's Mr. Robby and baby Signe."

Kylie darts up and runs barefoot toward them. I watch as she wraps her arms around Robby's leg and then looks in the stroller. Our eyes meet, and he walks toward us. Sometimes I forget that he and I have a niece in common. As Robby gets closer, I hear Signe crying and stand up to check on her.

"What's wrong, baby girl?" I take Signe out of the stroller. "Is your uncle being mean to you? Is his fancy shirt rubbing against your sensitive skin?"

Robby rakes his hand through his hair and exhales. "She's been crying since Jake and Camilla walked out the door. I don't know what to do, but I'd hate to make them leave their date early. They never get out."

I hold Signe close against me and pat her behind. "Shh, Signe. Everything's okay. You're fine. Your favorite Auntie Jenna is here now."

"Nice, Jenna." Robby shakes his head.

Signe continues to scream. "Have you fed her?" I look to Robby, who stands with his hands on his face.

"She wouldn't take the bottle Camilla left. I've tried her pacifier and a sound machine and even checked to ensure she didn't have string wrapped around a toe from her pajamas."

Kylie looks on with concern. "It's okay, Signe. It's okay."

"Where's her bottle?" I turn to Dax again, and he grabs it from the diaper bag and hands it to me.

"Did you test the milk?"

Dax freezes, and he raises an eyebrow. He leans in and says close to my ear. "That's breast milk. Am I supposed to drink my sister's breast milk?"

I pull back, and he's so serious that I feel bad for giving him a hard time. "I was joking, Robby."

Signe fusses when I move her to a lying position and keep her moving. I put the bottle up to her, and at first, her bottom lip pushes it away, but then she concedes, and smacks away.

Robby looks relieved. I am too. It's quiet for the first time since Robby approached us. I look down at Signe. Her blinks get longer as she fights sleep.

"Jenna," Robby says. He stands next to me and looks down at Signe. "What was I doing wrong?"

"It's a hard age." Robby rubs his eyes. "My mom always told me this was the age I started having stranger danger. I'm sure that's all this is."

Robby peeks down at her. "But I'm her uncle."

"My mom also told me I went through a stage as a baby where I didn't like men, including my dad. Don't take it personally."

"So, I didn't ruin her?" Robby looks concerned and rubs a finger over one of Signe's hands.

I shield Signe's face from the sun. "You're doing great, but you're not her mom or dad, and sometimes babies just like women more at this age."

Robby shakes his head. "Dax and Carrie should have had me watch Kylie, and you, Signe."

"You're not Kylie's uncle," I remind him.

Robby picks Kylie up, and she rubs her hands over the stubble across his face. "Kylie, I don't think I should be left alone with this baby. Would you and Carrie come with me to Jake and Camilla's? You could help me babysit your cousin."

"Yes," Kylie says, and then moves to a whisper. "Can we, Auntie Jenna? Please?"

Robby sticks out his lip and pouts, and Kylie puts her cheek against Robby's, and I know there is no saying no.

"Fine," I finally say.

Kylie and Robby give each other a fist bump, and Signe squawks when I place her in the stroller. I put a pacifier in her mouth, and she falls back asleep. Kylie runs ahead, leading us to Jake and Camilla's.

"Jenna. Thank you." I look at Robby, and he takes his first deep breath since running into me today. "I've never been alone with a baby. Maybe I'm not ready to be. What were they thinking?"

"Where are Jake and Camilla, anyway?"

"At this new winery in Gracetown, I guess."

I nod. "That's where Dax and Carrie are too."

Robby lets out a bark. "It must have been a couples-only thing. I love a winery, but sure, I'll watch your screaming baby."

Robby kicks a rock down the road and then turns to me. "Your article on me was great. You made me seem not as boring as I am. Very multidimensional."

"Ahh, Robby." We look at each other. "It was a hard job, but someone had to do it. And you're not entirely boring. I sprinkled in some untruths, but no one will ever know."

He winks at me. "Well, thanks."

"Don't get a big head," I say. "A few Wheaton ladies have contacted the paper asking about you."

Robby playfully nudges my shoulder. "Not likely."

"I figured you'd be happy that I didn't divulge all of your secrets."

Robby laughs. "The chance that anyone from Goldman Sachs would ever read this newspaper is slim, but you never know. And until I have something lined up, I have to play the part of a committed employee who would never walk away. So, thank you."

We watch as Kylie skips several feet in front of us. She bends over, picks up a stick on the gravel road, and uses it for support. The air feels thick between us, but the ice thaws with each interaction. We avoid the hard topics but always find a million other things to discuss.

"What is next, Robby?" Curiosity finally forces me to ask the question weighing on my mind so heavily.

He turns to me. "There's this thing." Robby pauses.

"Go on." I nod.

He shakes his head. "And it's so out of left field, but also intriguing, and I don't know, I've been considering exploring it."

"I'm dying to know."

"A friend of mine from Wharton started this organization called Teaching America. It's really taken off the past few years, and he reached out to me recently to see if I have any interest."

He peers down at a still sleeping Signe and then looks at me. "It's a non-profit, and their goal is to make education more accessible for all Americans, especially those from marginalized communities."

We reach Jake and Camilla's house, and Kylie walks inside. I fear waking Signe up, so instead, I sit at a table and keep her stroller moving.

"Khalif, my friend, is amazing, and yeah," Robby continues, "he wants to bring me on. I'd join their board, but he also wants to deploy me into the classroom. I'm a finance guy, and they desperately need help in that area."

Robby sits beside me, and I hold his gaze. "Wow."

"Now that I've said it out loud." He closes his eyes and shakes his head. "It's stupid, isn't it?"

"It's not that." I study Robby. "This is the first time I've seen your eyes light up since you got to Wheaton."

He turns his head and opens his mouth only slightly. "I didn't realize eyes could smile."

"Yours can." I've said too much. I always do. I can't help myself. It's one of my worst traits. "Someday, I hope a man talks about me like you talk about Teaching America."

Robby smiles and lays his hand flat on the picnic table. "So, it doesn't sound like the most ridiculous idea you've ever heard of?"

"It sounds amazing." I look down at Signe as she starts to stir. "Tell me more."

"They are headquartered in Chicago but are looking for more boots on the ground. If I sign up, I could end up anywhere across the United States, and that scares the shit out of me."

I hate the ease I fall back into with him. I've been convinced since I reacquainted with him two summers ago that I could never think of Robby as only a friend. Talking to him makes me want to learn more. However, I feel like I'm teetering on the edge of the cliff, ready to fall, and knowing I should grab someone's hand to anchor me.

Something about him draws me in, and no matter how much I want to put up walls, I lose my armor around him.

"What's your gut telling you?" I lean back on one of my elbows.

Robby runs his hands through his hair. "That I didn't learn finance to sit in an ivory tower and help rich people get richer."

"And," I lean forward. "What's the practical part of you staying?"

"That the base salary for a position with Teaching America is equaled to only one of my two annual bonuses."

I raise my eyebrows.

"Sorry, Jenna. But you asked."

Kylie peeks through the door and, in her loudest voice, says, "Aren't you guys coming inside?"

Signe stirs and then full-on screams. I pick her up, which helps, but only a little. Robby looks at me and puts his hand on my shoulder. The touch makes it hard to breathe, but even more difficult is the look he gives me.

"I miss this." Robby points at me and then at himself. "A lot."

Robby turns from me and walks inside, and Kylie holds the door open. I follow them, but I'm not sure what to say. The truth is that I miss Robby's friendship too. I'm not even mad at him anymore for what happened in the past. I know myself and how on the verge of being in love with him I am. I also know that our lives are taking us in different directions and that I can't have distractions as I plan out the next stage of my life.

WHEN BABYSITTING IS DONE, I drive back to town. My conversation with Robby replays in my head. I have flashbacks of him on the floor with Kylie, playing a card game, as I soothed Signe.

I pull around back, like I always do, and park my car in the safety of the garage, so Eli will never know where I live. I close the garage door, and then pull my keys out of my purse.

"Jenna."

The moment I hear my name, the breath gets stuck in my throat, and options run through my head. Do I take off running, or do I speak to him, and hope it's the last time that will rid me of him once and for all?

"Eli." I turn to him but recoil. He's massive and intimidating, and as I look at him, I can't remember why I ever gave dating him a shot.

He takes a step closer, and I hold out my arm. "Don't you dare come closer."

"Jenna." He then tucks his arms at his side. "Give me another chance. If it doesn't work out, then I'll walk away. Forever. I love you, Jenna. I know we can work this out."

I've never conversed with someone as clueless as Eli.

It doesn't matter what I say. He doesn't get it. I always find myself trying to attach logic to a place and person where it ceases to exist. I'm becoming wiser, and nothing I say to him will ever make him realize that this is not love but harassment.

"Eli." I exhale. "I'm only going to say this once more because I've already said it a hundred times. You need to leave me alone. Move on. Your presence makes me uncomfortable. You're everywhere."

His face wrinkles, and his body tenses. "I'm not doing anything illegal. We're in an alley. I'm not on your property."

He knows the laws, and of course, he does. "I'm not accusing you of doing anything illegal. You need to let go. I'm done. You need to be too."

"I love you, Jenna," Eli says, stepping back.

"You don't." I turn my back to him and walk to the door.

He grabs my arm and turns me toward him. His eyes darken when he speaks his next words. "I don't want you to do something you will regret."

Eli removes his hand from me, walks to his car, which then squeals off.

Chapter Ten

Robby

CAMILLA AND GRANDMA SIS ENTER an apple pie in the contest for Wheaton Days, and Sunny, Jake and I head to the festival to cheer them on. I push Signe in a stroller, and she's out cold. Sleeping babies are my favorite version of babies at the moment.

"I hope Sis doesn't get overwhelmed." Sunny looks at me as we reach the judging area. "She doesn't do so well when she gets out of her routine."

"Let's make sure we don't stay long." We reach the main stage. "Right after judging, we'll get Sis home so she can take an afternoon nap."

Sunny waves at Annie and Walt on the other side of the street. "Will you go to the street dance tonight? I hear the band is supposed to be good."

"Maybe for a bit," Jake says.

"Not me," I respond. "I'm going to sit this one out."

A person walks up on stage, saying they'll announce the pie competition next.

"I invited the group out to the cottage, though. I

thought it would be fun to host something. The kids are sleeping at Mr. and Mrs. Abrams."

Sunny smiles. "I love that. The cottage is meant to be enjoyed. I can't tell you how many card games we played with Oscar and Eleanor Abram. Such happy memories."

We watch Sis and Camilla get first place in the pie competition because I don't think anyone could beat Grandma Sis's apple pie. The rest of the festivities are geared toward kids, so I head back to the cottage, and Jake and Camilla head home with Signe. Everyone will come by later after enjoying the street dance for an hour or so. I have no interest in hearing the band this year. The only people I know in Wheaton are couples, and standing around awkwardly, and drinking beer out of a plastic cup, doesn't do much for me. Not anymore.

I find myself relishing the newfound freedom that came from my break from Goldman Sachs. For the first time in my life, I have no job waiting for me, no pressing responsibilities or tasks to complete. It's a strange feeling, like stepping into an uncharted territory of possibilities. I know that at some point, I will have to decide whether to return to my career at Goldman Sachs.

For now, I'm content to simply relax, and wait for my friends to arrive. The music blares through the speakers, and I feel the rhythm and melody pulse through my body. I crack open a cold beer, savoring the refreshing taste on my tongue. As I sit outside, the warmth of the sun kissing my skin and a gentle breeze in my hair, I can't help but feel a sense of liberation and contentment.

Camilla and Jake pull up first, and even though I told her not to bring anything, she has a tray of something in her hands. Camilla struggles to open the door with her hands full, and I jump to my feet to help.

"Hey, Robby. I'm baby-free for the next twelve hours. I am going to drink so much wine and sleep in so late tomorrow."

Dax and Carrie arrive next, with Jenna. Carrie has a bowl of something she hands me as well.

"I love Signe, don't get me wrong," Jake says as he grabs a water and pulls up a chair. "I am going to sleep in so late tomorrow. And I won't feel guilty about it."

The clouds move in quickly, and then there's a large roar of thunder, and we all pause for a moment, looking at each other. And then rain pours out of the skies, and we all run inside the cottage.

"It always rains during Wheaton Days, I swear." Camilla says as she pulls a couple of bottles of wine out of the fridge. "This is the third summer in a row it's poured during the street dance."

"Good thing we opted out then." Dax walks behind Carrie and wraps his arms around her.

Camilla then digs through her bag and pulls something out. She puts it on the table and starts clapping her hands. Jenna goes to investigate what it is.

"Truth or drink?" Jenna says, holding up the game and reading the back. "Is the game as self-explanatory as the name?"

"It's supposed to be fun," Camilla says, and then looks at Jake, "And of course, you can drink anything of your choice, including non-alcoholic things."

Jake shakes his head. "I'll play, but if Jenna gets any questions about sex, she has to drink because, as far as I'm concerned, she's still a virgin."

"Nice," Jenna says and punches Jake in the arm, and he puts her in a head lock and messes up her hair.

"Ironically," I say. "My sister is also still a virgin, which I know is complicated by the fact that she did, in fact, birth a child, but the same goes for questions for Camilla. There will be no sex questions."

Camilla and Jenna exchange a look and shake their

heads. Carrie pours the three girls a glass of wine and looks at Jake and me. "You men are sexist. Do you think your sisters want to think of you guys as anything but virgins? Doubt it."

"Alright, let's play," Camilla says, and we all sit around the table.

I rolled my eyes more than anyone when Camilla suggested playing this game, but it's more funny than scandalous, and we're all laughing and feeling good. Being around all of these people is good for Jenna, and me too. It provides a layer of protection and shows that we can be in the same company and not have it be a big deal, which has been the goal all along.

Jenna takes the next card on the table and shakes her head. We've implemented the rule that even if someone decides to drink instead of answering the question, they still have to read the card.

Jenna glances down and reads. "How many people in the room would you be willing to kiss?" She looks up, and her eyes dart to mine, but then she looks away. "Well, two of you are my brothers, and Camilla and Carrie, you're pretty and all, but you kiss my brothers, and I think that's gross. Which only leaves Robby."

All eyes look at me, and I smile. "So, your answer is one?"

Jenna purses her lips, pauses, and then puts the card down. "I'll drink."

Everyone laughs, and Jenna's eyes flick to mine over her wine glass as she takes a sip. She'd rather drink than answer a question about being willing to kiss me.

Now it's my turn. I grab the card and immediately want a new one. I go to put it back.

Dax reaches his hand across the table. "The rules, Robby. You have to read it."

"Have you ever cheated in a relationship?" I let out a

long sigh. Of all the questions I could have gotten, I had to get this one in front of Jenna.

I grab my glass and take a drink. Camilla stands up and swats my arm. "Robby, you pig."

Sober Camilla would have read my body language and not pushed it, but after two glasses of wine, Camilla missed the signals entirely. I wave her away, and Dax saves the day by grabbing a card and reading the next question. I avoid looking at Jenna. I don't want to see her face.

The game continues, and when my turn comes around, I keep getting the worst cards.

"Have you ever kissed someone in this room?" Drink.

I read the next card. "What's the biggest lie you've ever told?" Does omission count as a lie? Of course it does, and I drink again.

"What is your longest dry spell?" Seeing that I recently hit over two years, not that I'm keeping track, I think I'll drink again.

By the time the game ends, everyone except for Jenna and me is remarkably sober. It's as if someone handpicked the questions for the two of us, and every card was something that we most definitely did not want to share with each other.

"Who wants to drive Jenna home?" Dax asks, and he and Jake stare at each other, hoping the other one will do it.

No one speaks up. Jenna leans forward and rests her face in her hands. "Don't everyone volunteer at once."

Jake looks at Camilla, and it's a look I know well, and I almost throw up in my mouth. They are childless for the night and have some things in mind that they'd want to do. Then Dax gives Carrie a similar look.

Jenna goes to stand but then sits again. "You two are

the worst brothers. The worst." She folds her arms over her chest.

"You can stay in the guest room if you want." I point to the room. "The bedding is clean."

All eyes are on me. Camilla nods. "It's a nice room. A comfortable bed."

Jenna looks at me. "It seems like this is the only option, right Jake? Dax?"

"Great, it's settled." Jake pulls his keys out of his pocket and holds them up for Camilla. They can't get out of here fast enough.

"I'll take care of her and make sure she gets to bed."

Jake looks at me with hooded eyes. "You better. Call you tomorrow, Jenna." Jake kisses her cheek, and then the four of them leave.

"They're the worst." Jenna stands and then leans against the table to steady herself.

I hold up a finger to her and then walk to the room I'm staying in. I go through the drawer and grab a shirt and shorts. I put them on the table for her.

Jenna holds up the shirt and then the shorts. "Even your pajamas are preppy."

"They aren't my pajamas. They're my workout clothes." I go into the fridge and grab a bottle of water.

Jenna laughs. "I correct myself. Even your workout clothes are preppy."

We stand only a foot apart, and she holds my clothes close to her chest. She shakes her head. "That game was not fun."

"It's like they set us up." I bark a laugh.

"I wouldn't put it past them." Jenna glances at the clothes in her hand.

"Your questions were almost as bad as mine."

Jenna leans against the table but sways. I reach my hand up and grab her around her elbow, steadying her.

"Well, Robby." Jenna pouts her lips out and blinks. "I now see three of you, which is my sign that it's time for bed."

"Let me know if you need anything." I start shutting off the lights throughout the cottage. "You know where the bathroom is. There's a lot more water in the fridge, and extra blankets in the closet if you get cold. Which you won't, because the cabin doesn't have air conditioning so it's never cold in here."

"Okay." Jenna turns and walks into the guest room and closes the door behind her.

Chapter Eleven

Jenna

Two Years Ago

CHICAGO WAS ON MY SHORTLIST of places to go to journalism school, so when Robby suggested I come for a long weekend and he'd give me a tour of the city, I jumped at the opportunity. I'd never been there before, and as the plane flew over the city, I couldn't get over how big it was. Buildings stretched out in every direction.

My phone dinged when we landed. Robby let me know he was going to meet me by ground transportation. He didn't trust that I could navigate my way to his apartment building alone. He was probably right.

When I saw him standing there, I could barely catch my breath. I'd never seen this side of Robby before. He stood at the bottom of the escalator, and still hadn't seen me. He wore a fitted suit, charcoal gray, with a crisp white shirt and dark tie underneath. Robby looked important and like he belonged here. I looked down at myself and was underwhelming in comparison.

When he saw me, his eyes lit up, and his smile widened. I reached the bottom of the escalator, and we hugged each other in a slightly pensive embrace. Perhaps things wouldn't be as natural as they were when we were in Wheaton together. Chicago Robby was a guy that I didn't know.

He gazed at me.

"What is it?" I looked down at my outfit again.

Robby grabbed my rolling bag. "You're so out of context here. Sorry, I'll quit staring." He shook his head and laughed.

He ordered us a car service into the city, and we reached his Lake View building. We got into the elevator and stopped on the eighth floor.

"I rented one of our guest suites for you for the weekend. My place is a one-bedroom, so I thought this would be more comfortable."

"Yeah. No." I stammered. "Of course."

I hid a lot in my expression. Like, the fantasy of Robby finally making a move while we were here and seeing the city on his arm after spending a night enjoying each other's bodies. Yes, women had fantasies too, and when Robby invited me to Chicago, I thought that this short weekend away meant something for us.

He got off the elevator with me and brought me to the guest suite. It was nice. Modern.

"It has everything you'll need. Coffee maker. Fresh towels, and if you think of something else, let me know. I probably have it."

Robby walked to the door. "Do you want to see my place?"

"Great." I followed him.

Robby scanned his card to get up to the thirty-third floor. Only four rooms were on this floor, and we entered his. The condo was an expansive, open space. The kitchen opened to the living space. The floors were dark wood, and everything else was in shades of white and gray.

One entire wall was a sliding glass door. He opened it, and it revealed the perfect view of Lake Michigan. A grill outside, which he informed me he never uses, and two chairs. He then showed me his bedroom. A massive king bed, the largest walk-in closet I've ever seen, and an en suite bathroom with a stand-up shower and a soaker tub.

I first walked out of his bedroom and turned back to look at him. "Coming to Wheaton must feel like slumming it?"

He smiled. "This place was a great investment." Robby leaned in and whispered. "I'm actually not this fancy."

I didn't believe him, though. Because this place was extravagant and pristine, and Robby fit in here.

"It looks like you haven't even moved in," I said. "There are no pictures or personality. Nothing."

"Yeah," Robby shrugged. "I haven't figured out what I want this place to look like yet."

Robby loosened his tie. "Here's the plan. I need to finish a bit more work, but we have reservations at eight. Do you like Filipino food?"

"Maybe." I shrugged my shoulders.

Robby pulled his tie over his head, took his suit coat off, and unbuttoned the top button of his dress shirt. He looked as relieved as I was when I took my bra off as soon as I got home from being in public.

"I've never had it," I admitted.

"I think you'll like it," Robby said. "I'll come to your room a little before eight and get you. You can freshen up, shower, do whatever."

It turned out Filipino food was amazing. Robby let me know that I was mainly on my own on Friday because he had a lot of work to do, and I hid my disappointment. He promised to spend all Saturday with me. Chicago Robby was a lot different from the one I'd come to know this summer. He was serious. Busy. Driven. Responsible. In Wheaton, everything about him felt more spontaneous.

I woke up on Friday to a text from Robby telling me he was already at work and that he'd meet me for dinner and drinks at seven. This was not the Chicago experience I expected. I thought Robby would clear his calendar and introduce me to his friends, but I spent the day alone. I had my day all mapped out, I had meetings at two universities with journalism programs, as well as some shopping.

I started my day at DePaul University and met with someone in admissions. From there, I headed over to Loyola. I walked around the city, took selfies at Navy Pier, and then hit the stores.

Robby told me the name of the downtown restaurant I was meeting him at, and I looked at the website and menu. The prices were insane, as in, I'd never had a meal for that much in my life. This restaurant also required me to bring one of my nicer dresses, a beautiful emerald-green silk dress with an almost completely open back.

After showering and getting ready back in my guest room, I headed over to the restaurant. As I walked through the doors, Robby texted me again to wait for him at the bar and that he was on his way. I always thought Fridays were supposed to be an easier day at work, but Robby must have put in twelve hours.

The entire restaurant was darkly lit, and I took a spot at the bar and ordered myself a cosmopolitan. It seemed like the right atmosphere for that. A man sat next to me, and we made eye contact.

"Hello." He offered and held his glass up to mine. His accent was thick, and I couldn't tell if it was Irish or Scottish.

Did he want me to toast him? I held mine up too.

He held my gaze and then smiled. "I have to ask, are you meeting someone here?"

"I am." I nodded. "My friend."

His eyes perked up like this somehow would give him a chance with me, and I regretted offering that bit of information up immediately.

"A friend. So, you're saying I have a chance?" He ran his hand through his ginger beard.

I politely smiled. "Well, I'm not from here—"

"No one is from here, darling. I'm Garret." The man held his hand out to me.

"Umm, hi. Jenna." I shook his hand.

I didn't see Robby approach, but his fingers grazed my arm, before they settled on my wrist. He leaned in and kissed my cheek. "Sorry, I'm late. Our table is ready."

Robby looked at me, then glanced at Garret and back at me. He acted as if he was seeing me for the first time, and his gaze lingered long enough for goosebumps to fill my body.

Garret smiled. "Have a lovely evening, Jenna. With your friend."

We sat down and looked at each other from across the table. "You look stunning, Jenna."

So did he. This time in a navy-blue suit. He took his suit coat off and rolled the sleeves of his button up, exposing his forearms. My face filled with heat.

"Casual Fridays must not be a thing in Chicago."

He laughed. Hard. Like I'd said the funniest thing he'd ever heard.

Robby leaned his elbows on the table. "How long were you alone at that bar, and how many numbers did you get, Jenna Abram?"

Our server came by, and I ordered another Cosmo.

Robby ordered a Manhattan.

"No numbers, I'm afraid." I glanced back at the bar. "I was close though."

He raised an eyebrow. "How are you single?"

"Well," I said. "It's slim pickings in Wheaton. What's your excuse? Chicago is full of beautiful people."

Robby brushed his hand along his jaw, moved it to the back of his neck, and closed his eyes as he squeezed. When he opened his eyes again, he looked at me. His lips turned up ever so slightly, but then he changed the subject.

"The Wagyu rib eye is to die for."

I opened my menu. The first thing I saw was the price. I glanced at Robby over my menu. "Are you avoiding my question, Robby Bergland?"

He took a long and audible sigh. "It's complicated."

"Hmm." I rested my chin on my hand.

"What?" Robby said.

"And here I thought we talked about everything."

He didn't elaborate though, and I didn't push it. Instead, I spent the rest of the evening curious about what "complicated" meant in Robby's life.

Saturday, I got Robby all to myself. He came by around nine with bagels he picked up around the corner, and we decided to play tourists for the day. Well, Robby decided to play tourist. I was a tourist. We did the lookout at the Sears Tower and then took a boat on an architectural tour. We rode the Ferris wheel at Navy Pier and got our photo taken in one of those photo booths. Today was the first day I recognized Robby as the guy I'd gotten to know. He let loose again.

After a full day, we ended up at his place, and ordered Chinese takeout, and I insisted on paying because last night's dinner that he paid for was not cheap. We sat out on his balcony, feet resting on the railing.

"Well, Jenna." Robby looked at me. "Could you see yourself here?"

"The schools were great." I forked rice onto my plate. "It's not far from home. There are hot guys with accents. A definite contender."

"There is no competing with an accent. Although for whatever reason, when I lived overseas with my family, women didn't dig my accent."

We sat in silence for a moment and looked out at the lake we could no longer see due to the darkness. I finally broke the silence.

"Hey." Our eyes met, and he pulled his lips into his mouth to wet them. "You're different in Chicago."

"What do you mean?"

"In Wheaton, I feel like I know who you are." I took my feet off the railing and crossed my legs. "But, here, you're like this buttoned-upped version of yourself."

Robby closed his eyes for a mere second. "You're different here too."

"Me?" I pointed to myself. "I feel the same."

Robby put his plate down and turned to me. "Last night, I watched you at the bar for a few moments before approaching you. It was hard for me to connect you with the person I've gotten to know in Wheaton."

"Hmm." I rubbed my lips together. "Which version do you like better?"

"Well, the version of you from Wheaton is attainable." Robby rubbed his hands together. "But that woman I saw at the bar last night, well, she's going to rule the world. And whoever she'll allow into her orbit will be a lucky son of a bitch."

My mouth opened, but nothing came out.

Later that night, Robby walked me to the eighth floor. We rode the elevator down in silence, and I pondered friendships between male and female. I grew up with so many guy friends, but maybe those relationships only worked when there wasn't any attraction.

At times, Robby said things to me that were so amazingly kind, that his words took my breath away. But he never crossed a line with me. Yet, my attraction to him was growing, and if he didn't feel similarly, it was going to make a future friendship challenging.

Chapter Twelve

Robby

Two Years Ago

$\mathcal{I}$ CAN'T REMEMBER THE LAST TIME I spent the Fourth of July in Wheaton. It was probably when I was an early teenager, my dad was between assignments, and we had time during the summer to spend stateside.

But when I was here for Wheaton Days, everyone was talking about the Fourth of July weekend, and on a whim, I decided to come here for a few nights for the holiday weekend.

At times, I felt like I was watching my life unfold as a stranger, floating overhead. In my entire life, I'd never been to Wheaton twice in the same summer, yet here I was. And I'd love to say it was because I missed my grandparents, or my sister, but I knew what the pull was. I knew who drew me here.

Wheaton had become a refuge. I came here and could ignore all the things I needed to change about my life at home. Nothing needed to be faced here. I knew I was pushing my problems to the future, and at some point, I'd have to deal with them, but not today.

Chicago was dead this weekend, anyway. Everyone fled the city in search of cabins, get-togethers, and small-town festivals. I'd spent many July Fourth weekends in Chicago, and I felt like I almost had the city to myself. A lot of people in my friend group were driving up to Wisconsin to go to a rented cabin, but nothing sounded better than spending the weekend with my sister and grandparents.

The morning of the fourth, I woke up in my grandparents' guest bedroom, me in one twin bed and Camilla in the other. The cottage still wasn't ready, so when I visited, I resorted to sleeping arrangements with my little sister like when we were younger. She was out, and I stood over her, and watched her sleep. She must have felt my presence because her eyes darted open.

"What are you doing, Robby? You look like a crazy person."

I laughed and threw a pillow at Camilla's head. "It's the Fourth of July weekend. Wake up."

"So what? I'm tired." Camilla moaned into her pillow.

She looked at me, but then her eyes were reduced to slits. "Fine, Camilla, but I promised Jenna and Dax I would pick a few things up to run to Jake's. It sounds like it will be a big crowd. Should you and I drive separately?"

Camilla stretched over to the nightstand and looked at her phone. "Yes. I want to spend a little time with Grandma and Grandpa first and then run a few things to the cottage so I can sleep there tonight. I'll meet you at some point."

After picking up a few items from the grocery store, I drove out to Jake's house. I was one of the first to arrive, and Jenna was the first person I saw. She was on the lawn, setting up a volleyball court, in nothing but her bikini. Before she saw me, I stared. Or maybe I was gawking. In my mind, I'd already crossed the line of an appropriate male, female relationship, and I needed to be honest with her, people back home, and myself, but instead, I walked further into this thing with her.

I composed myself and opened my car door. Jenna heard the car door slam when I closed it, looked up from what she's doing, and waved to me.

"Robby," she said, jogging to me. "You're here, and just in time. I need some help setting up."

Side by side, we helped Jake get everything ready. And it wasn't too long before people started showing up. It was a hot summer day, and Dax came and stood by us.

"Hey," he said, and put a hand on my back. "Do you want to take the jet skis out?"

For whatever reason, I appreciated the diversion. "Let's do it, man."

Dax and I put on our life jackets and headed across the lake. We both put them in full throttle, and the wind blew in my hair and I felt free. We reached a small pile of rocks in the water, and we slowed to almost a stop.

"How are you doing?" I killed the engine and looked at Dax. "And Kylie?"

Dax killed his engine too and rested his head on the handlebars. "Kylie honestly seems great. She's mostly happy. I have her see a therapist though. She's so adjusted. Maybe too adjusted."

"And you?" I asked.

Dax let out a breath. "I have good days and bad days. And lately, mostly bad days."

The waves of another jet ski pushed us more toward the South Dakota shore, but we kept our engines off.

"Do you think you'll ever date again?"

Dax looked at me and shook his head. "I think a love like Zari and I had comes around once in a lifetime."

We got in shallow water, so I turned the engine on to

get us further out. Dax did the same.

"Some people go through life never finding their person. But I found mine," Dax said. "I'd be open to dating, someday, but the thought that I could ever love someone the way I loved Zari, well, it doesn't seem possible."

We maintained a slow speed, side by side, and then Dax looked at me. He blew out a breath, but then said, "Do you have a thing for my sister?"

"No," I said, too quickly. Then I coughed, caught off guard by the question. "Jenna is great. We've gotten close, but—"

"Don't hurt her," Dax said, interrupting me.

"No, of course not," I shook my head. "I have no intentions of hurting her."

"Jenna acts all tough, but she's sensitive." Dax turned his jet ski to head back to Jake's house. "And I shouldn't say this, because she'd kill me, but I think she has a bit of a crush on you."

My face reddened, and I kept my eyes straight forward so Dax couldn't see it. That's what I was afraid would happen, which is why I needed to talk to her tonight. I needed to tell her everything and hoped she'd still let me be in her life. I always planned to say something earlier in the summer, but then time kept passing, and it didn't seem natural to bring things up as the more time passed.

"I'm not in a place—" I began to say.

"Don't tell me, tell Jenna."

We got back to Jake's, and Jenna found me.

"There you are. You were gone so long." Jenna looked at me. "Do you want to go to my favorite place to watch the fireworks?"

It was getting dark. "Umm, sure."

She took my hand. "It's at the point."

We walked down the gravel road to the point, and Jenna turned to me. "When I was little, we'd climb rocks from my grandparents' lake home to Sunny and Sis's cottage. Grandpa Oscar always packed me a peanut butter and butter sandwich, which are far superior to peanut butter and jelly."

Our hands were intertwined, and Jenna's face lit up as she continued her story. "We'd stop on this rock, which was about the halfway point, and Grandpa and I would sit on the rock, and he'd pull out my wrapped sandwich from his pocket."

The sun got darker in the sky, and Jenna smiled. We sat together on the large, flat rock. Our feet rested on many of the smaller rocks that surround it. "He named it Jenna's rock. And I don't know, it remains my favorite and I love to come out here and sit and think."

Jenna wrapped her arm around me, and we sat, my thigh rubbed against hers. We stayed silent for a while, and watched the explosion of colors overhead, and the roaring thunder that made the rock underneath me vibrate. And then instead of watching the fireworks, I stared at Jenna.

She looked so young as she smiled at the sky. She caught me looking. My eyes glanced at Jenna's lips, and I knew she saw me. I squeezed my eyes shut, and when I open them, she was still watching me. I knew what I must do when I got back to Chicago. I inched forward, and the fireworks faded into the distance. I was inches from her face, testing. Probing. She smelled like lilacs and sunblock, but I couldn't kiss her. Not here. Not until I took care of things at home. At the last second, I turned my head, and kissed her cheek.

Jenna sat still and didn't say a thing. She inhaled and held the breath in her chest for several seconds, before she released it. "Let's head back to Jake's," she finally said.

We got into one of Jake's guest rooms, and Jenna had

already put an extra mattress on the floor for me. She went into the bathroom to shower, and I looked around the room. I needed to put distance between us, or I would catch feelings that I wouldn't be able to stop. I couldn't have that happen.

I had a life back in Chicago and people that would be hurt if I crossed a boundary here. Jenna walked through the door with clothes she threw at me and told me they're Jake's.

Jenna jumped into the bed and pulled the covers over her. I've realized this summer that I'd never had a female friendship like the one I had with Jenna. I'd never had a friendship like this at all. And I wanted to protect it at all costs, which is why I needed to push down the growing attraction I had for her.

"How long after you broke off your engagement before you moved on?" I laid my head back and rested them on my folded hands.

Jenna moved to her side and placed her head on her hand. The light was dim, but I could perfectly make out her features.

"I mean, I still haven't really seriously dated since." Jenna chewed on her lip and then looked at me. "But imagine spending your entire life with someone because it was too hard to end it."

I shifted to my side as well. "But what does happy even look like? I feel like all of that fades at some point."

Jenna put her head on her pillow. "I told you how low my expectations are. Sex without socks."

"Jenna." I sat up. I was starting to think that Jenna brought humor to situations, so she didn't have to discuss the hard things. "We seriously need to discuss raising your standards."

Jenna sat up too. "What are your baseline requirements for someone you're dating?"

"Besides no socks during sex?" I grinned. "Someone who wants to spend the day with me and not text me 'hey you up' for a booty call. A girl who wants to know my family because they're important to me. Someone who will hold my hand and hug me in public."

Jenna pulled her lips into a thin line. "You just described every girl I know. Maybe I'm not the only one who needs higher standards."

I opened my mouth, and what I needed to tell Jenna was on the tip of my tongue. She watched me as if she knew I had something to say, but no matter how hard I tried and how much I knew it was the right thing to do, I couldn't get myself to do it. Instead, I leaned over and turned off the light.

"Goodnight, Jenna."

Chapter Thirteen

Jenna

IT'S A HOT SUMMER DAY, and Wheaton is decorated in red, white, and blue. Main Street has been transformed. The ground vibrates underneath me as the band warms up and prepares to be in the annual Fourth of July parade. I fan myself with one of my hands, which provides little reprieve.

Camilla, Carrie, and I said we'd bring the kids to the parade while the men got ready for the party that Jake and Camilla are having after the parade.

"Signe," Camilla says, kissing her cheeks. "You'll have so much fun sleeping at Grandma and Grandpa's tonight."

Kylie leans over and holds Signe's hand. "I'll be there too, so it will be okay."

Carrie squeezes Kylie. "You're such a little mama, Kylie."

Kylie beams. "Someday, maybe I'll have a baby sister."

Carrie, Camilla, and I look at each other, eyes raised, and burst out laughing.

"Speaking of babies," I say. "When are you and Dax going to get married? You said you wanted a short engagement."

Carrie looks at Kylie, and they both smile. "Should we tell them, Kylie?"

Kylie claps her hands together. "Yes."

"As you know, Dax and I want it super small. I'm talking about twenty people or less." Carrie glances at me first, and then looks to Camilla.

"Yes." Camilla holds her hands up, impatiently waiting to hear more.

"Well." Carrie looks at us. "Jenna, we don't know where you're going to end up, and we don't want you to have to fly back for something. And the bed-and-breakfast is doing great, and well, there's no reason to delay."

"So," Camilla and I say in unison.

"So," Carrie draws out the word. "Late August. At our house."

We all stand up and hug while jumping around. Poor Signe is in a baby carrier on Camilla's chest and gets caught in our embrace. I lift Kylie so she can be part of it too.

"Best news ever." I give my soon-to-be sister-in-law one more hug.

AFTER THE PARADE AND THE festivities in town, I stop home and pack a bag, and then head to Jake and Camilla's place. Jake has held a party out here every year since he built this home, and once he and Camilla got together, they co-hosted the event. People drop in at their leisure, and the festivities always go late into the evening, well after the fireworks show. I change into my suit and find

Carrie.

"It's so hot." I fan myself, and Dax comes up and wraps his arms around her. "Do you guys want to swim out to the trampoline?"

"I'm game," Dax says, looking around. His eyes spot someone, and I turn around and see Robby approaching us. "Robby, you up for swimming to the trampoline?"

"Yes." Robby peels his shirt off. "It has to be more than a hundred degrees out here today."

When the Berglands would come to Wheaton every summer, we had alliances within our group. Jake hung out mostly with Robby and Camilla's cousin Liam. And then Dax, Robby, and their other cousin David were inseparable. As the only girls and the two youngest, Camilla and I did everything together. Dax and Robby have always kept in touch through the years too, so I have no right to roll my eyes when Dax goes out of his way to include Robby in everything.

Being with a shirtless Robby all day will not do anything to help my attraction to him. No. It does the opposite.

We swim the twenty yards to the water trampoline. Carrie climbs up the ladder first, followed by Dax. Robby motions for me to go up next, and I'm mindful that my butt is in his face as I climb it. When I reach the top, I sprawl out onto it, and the sun warms my body.

Dax lies down next to me. "It feels great to be here celebrating again. Last year, I missed the party. Kylie and I were in Atlanta."

Robby lies down next to Dax. "I wasn't here last year either. So, it's been two years for me too."

"Jenna and I were here," Carrie says.

Dax leans on his side and puts his open palm on her stomach. "I bet you were moping around. Sad that I wasn't around."

Carrie swats him. "You wish." She then lifts her head to kiss him.

"If you guys start making out, I'm out of here." I lean back on my elbows and pull Carrie toward me and away from my brother.

"Agreed." Robby covers his eyes from the sun.

"You guys are no fun." Dax stands up and pulls Carrie with him. "Want to take a dip?"

Before Carrie can respond, the two of them jump in the water. I flip onto my stomach and rest my head on my arms. "Those two are pathetic."

Robby laughs. "It's a little cute."

Robby flips too, and we're sunning our backs and facing each other.

"What's new in your world domination plan, Jenna?" Robby asks.

He's talking about my plan to get out of Wheaton. "I sent in five applications for master's in journalism programs. I should hear something in early August."

Robby reaches over and pulls me into a hug. We're skin to skin, and he is so warm and his body so firm. We're gradually slipping into the old pattern of friendship. The one that left me brokenhearted. The start of a new friendship feels like a slippery slope.

"That's awesome, Jenna. Tell me everything."

Robby lies on his side, focusing all of his attention on me, and I'm sure I can't breathe. "I cast a wide net in terms of prestige and locations. I applied to schools in Nashville, Chicago, Austin, New York, and Atlanta."

He presses his lips together and rubs his hand across his scruff. His facial hair, which is new this summer, is less beard and more five o'clock shadow.

"Those are all great options. Have you thought about where you want to be? What if you get into all of them?"

"I won't," I quickly say. "Yeah, I have a couple of favorites. These schools all have great documentary journalism programs, which I'm most interested in."

I sit up, and Robby follows. "And how about you? You're closer to thirty than I am. How's your plan to get out of investment banking going?"

His teeth scrape his bottom lip. "Well, you're the first I'm telling this to, but I submitted my application for Teaching America yesterday."

Robby shrugs like it's no big deal, but the smile that reaches his eyes gives himself away. I'm surprised at how excited I feel for him. He's felt so stuck and really dislikes what he does. I leap forward and practically tackle him, and he falls back, laughing.

"Robby." I compose myself and help him up, my hands still on his shoulders. "You did it? You decided to put your name in the hat?"

"I haven't gotten in yet," he adds. "And if I get the position, I'll have little to no say in where I end up. Which feels scary as hell."

Things continue to look up for both of us. I'm also aware that we are two passing ships in the night. I've already decided that even if I don't get into any of the five schools I applied to, I'm still going to move. I have to. My family is here, but my life isn't. And Robby has decided to put his fate in Teaching America, which could send him anywhere. I hope I don't have these strong feelings toward him forever. I'll find someone worthy at some point and move on from these suffocating feelings I have every time I think of Robby or am in his presence.

"Jenna." Robby's countenance changes. His look turns serious, and he looks down but then glances at me. "I need to tell you something."

"Okay." I nod.

"About what you said the other day." Robby pauses,

and my body suddenly feels cold and clammy. "About you not having a future and not seeming motivated."

"Robby." I put my hand up. "We don't need to do this."

"You didn't hear the entire conversation," Robby continues. "I told Camilla that you don't seem fully happy in Wheaton and wish you found the motivation to move on because I think you have a bright future ahead of you. But not here."

I think back to the conversation I overheard between Camilla and Robby. I'm honestly not sure exactly what I heard. I remember the word motivated. Wheaton. Future, or was it no future?

The trampoline shakes as Dax and Carrie climb up the ladder. Robby grips my arm. "You have to know I think more of you than that. Because I think the world of you."

Why is he saying these things to me? And why am I listening and thinking things are different from last time when he said all the right things and still shattered me?

"We're good." I nudge him in the arm. "About that point."

More people join us on the trampoline, and I take the opportunity to jump into the water and take a break from the sun. I go inside and change into dry clothes, then go into sister mode and start cleaning up the place. There are cans and used paper plates everywhere, so I walk around and tidy up.

The sun gets lower in the sky, and Jake starts a fire. I look around at everyone, trying to find the best place to watch the fireworks. The best view is from the water, but everyone seems to couple up, so I decide to go inside to grab a blanket, and I'll keep it simple this year and watch it from the grass.

I go into one of Jake and Camilla's guestrooms and

grab a blanket from the closet. The door creaks, and I turn around to see Eli standing there with a wrapped gift and card.

"Eli." I blow out a breath, and my arm hairs stand on edge. "What are you doing here?"

"Here." He holds out the box, but I shake my head.

"No. No," I say. I'm not sure how many times because, in my mind, it's all I'm saying. No. No. No. No. No, Eli, I don't want this attention from you. I don't want you to keep showing up. I hate how you make me feel. The majority of my thoughts stay in my head.

"Open it." Eli again gestures toward the box, and I back up, in a corner, with nowhere to go.

My body shakes, and I struggle to form words. "Eli." I start to say. I then inhale and blow out a breath. "You have to quit showing up everywhere I am. It's making me—"

"Jenna, wait," he says, stepping closer.

"No," I say once again. "You have to stop this."

"But I love you, Je—"

"Eli. No." I say, this time with more force. "Move on."

"I won't. I can't." Eli furrows his brow and tucks his monster hands into his pockets. He's so big and blocks the only exit.

"You have to." I press my body into the corner, hands against the wall.

"Carrie told me to grab you, the fire is . . ." Robby comes barreling into the room and stops when he sees me. He looks at me, Eli, and then back at me.

He sticks his hand out to Eli. "I'm Robby. I don't think we've officially met."

Eli shakes his hand. "Eli." And then he turns and leaves the room, without another word or glance.

The world around me blurs into an incomprehensible jumble of noise and light, as if my mind is unable to process anything. I slide down the wall until I hit the floor, my back pressed against the cool plaster. Pulling my knees to my chest, I wrap my arms around my legs and bury my face in my hands. Sobs wrack my body.

Robby appears at my side, and his presence is a comforting anchor in the midst of my overwhelming emotions. His strong arms enfold me in a warm hug. I shake uncontrollably, my tears soaking his shirt, and he continues to hold me firmly. He doesn't try to offer any words or platitudes, but simply holds me and lets me feel everything.

The fireworks explode outside, sending bright bursts of color and light cascading through the window. Robby calmingly touches my arm, and I feel a sense of safety and security. Gradually, my breathing slows, and the tears dry up. Robby loosens his grip, but continues to hold my shoulders, his presence a reassuring weight against me. "You're as white as a ghost." Robby rubs a finger down my arm. "Why the fuck does he keep showing up everywhere you're at?"

"Robby." I close my eyes.

He looks toward the door and then back at me. He lowers his voice to almost a whisper. "What'd he do to you?"

"Robby, no." I shake my head. I've never wanted this situation to have attention. I want to stick to my plan of leaving Wheaton, and Eli will fixate on someone else. Anyone else, which isn't fair to them. "It's not a big deal."

Robby picks up the box on the bed that Eli left behind. "Do you actually believe that?"

"No," I whisper the words. I know what this is, and it is a big deal. I feel violated and harassed. I've said in every way a person can say that I don't want him around me, yet he keeps coming back.

"Jenna." Robby puts my hair behind my ears and then rubs my shoulders. "You need to tell the police."

I close my eyes. "He is the police. He works in Rosso."

"Jenna." Robby pulls me into a hug again. "You're not going home tonight. You can't."

"It will be fine. Maybe if I just talk to him."

"No." Robby shakes his head. "It's escalating. You've told him to leave you alone, and he keeps coming back. He cornered you in this room. Who knows? Does Jake? Dax? Your parents?"

"No," I practically scream and get to my feet. "You can't say anything. I'm leaving soon. Maybe as early as September. Let it go."

Robby stands, too, and paces back and forth in the room. He rubs his face and pulls his lips into a thin line. He sits on the edge of the bed.

"Please don't go home tonight." Robby pats the bed beside him, and I sit. "I don't trust that guy."

"I'll stay." I don't tell Robby this, but I haven't felt safe at home since he showed up there. He knows where I live, and even though I'm unlisted, I'm sure it wasn't difficult for a cop to figure it out.

"I'm staying too." I go to protest, but Robby shakes his head. "If your brothers aren't aware of what this creep is doing to you, I'm not going to leave your side."

Chapter Fourteen

Robby

THIS MORNING, SUNNY AND SIS show up at the cottage with the usual suspects, Walt, Juan, and Lawson. The men want to throw a fishing line into the water. Grandma Sis and I sit under the shade of the big maple tree and watch them.

"You don't have to sit with me, Robby. Go join the men."

"I'm where I want to be." I put my hand on hers.

I've never been into fishing, hunting, or the other things my family has. I love being in Wheaton and the cottage, but only to visit. I couldn't imagine living here. I've always been more inclined toward the city. It's where I feel most comfortable. As a kid, I always felt uncomfortable being honest about this. I think my dad felt similarly to me. We all feel so much pressure to keep the traditions alive that we lose ourselves. I try to balance who I am while honoring how special the cottage is to all of us.

Sunny brings Sis out here a couple of times every week, and it's good for her to be here and to see this place.

"Do you want lemonade, Grandma? I have some inside."

"Oh dear, I've already had three glasses."

I smile politely. Grandma Sis hasn't had three glasses of anything to drink since being here, but I don't argue with her. It does no good. It's probably even better that she doesn't remember how much she forgets. If she remembered, she'd only feel shame. Even the last time I visited Wheaton, Grandma Sis knew how much she forgot or messed up details. It's almost better now because her Alzheimer's has progressed to a point where she isn't cognizant of all she's lost. Sadly, Grandma is happier in this state of her disease than she was in an earlier state.

"Got one," Sunny yells from the dock, and Walt grabs the net. "It's a walleye. At least eighteen inches, I do say."

Sunny holds the fish in his gloved hand, and the four of them walk to the fish cleaning table. Sunny holds the fish up to me. "Do you want to clean this one, Robby?"

"Not this time." I've gone almost thirty years not knowing how to fillet a fish, and there's no point in learning the art now, I figure.

"You should put a line in," Lawson calls toward me. "They are really starting to bite now."

After they leave, I go inside and look at the gift Eli brought Jenna. She didn't even realize I had taken it the next morning. I knew I recognized Eli when I saw him. He was the guy who showed up at closing time at The Pool Hall. I never introduced myself to him, but I had a bad feeling about him even then. My skin crawls in his presence. There is something not right with him.

The box sits on the kitchen table, and I put the card to the side and open the gift. It's a framed picture of Eli and Jenna and looks to be taken in the fall. They stand outside by a tree full of colorful leaves, and he puts his arm around her. I'm no body-language expert, but she didn't seem interested in him even then. Even in the photo, there is something in Jenna's expression that concerns me. She looks uncomfortable, yet it's even more than that.

I then move to the card. It's a handwritten note, and words sprinkle the page from front to back. Its content makes me sick. The sentiments aren't from someone well and healthy, but instead, they reek of delusion. He loves her. He'll always love her. He'll do anything to get her back. He won't take no for an answer. The letter then gets more explicit. He details all the things he wants to do with her sexually. Vomit feels like it comes up, almost escaping. I tuck the letter away in case it's needed as evidence for later. It's vile—all of it.

The most important thing to me is Jenna's safety. She was so adamant that I not say anything to her brothers, but no one, except for me now, knows what she's been going through. Jake and Dax are not men who mess around. If they knew what someone was putting their sister through, they'd react. I don't want to betray her trust, though. We're finally at a point where friendship seems like a possibility. She'd never speak to me again if I told Jake and Dax. But I'd never forgive myself if something happened to Jenna.

Last night, before falling asleep, I was on the floor, and Jenna in the bed, just like in the old days. I promised her I wouldn't tell anyone. I told her that if anything else happened, her family needed to know. I sit at my laptop and try to find everything I can about Eli. He's in his early thirties, has been part of the Rosso Police Department for ten years, and has rave reviews. Jenna can't be the only person he's done this to. There has to be a pattern with him, but my search comes up empty. The man has no social media presence.

I'm restless, so after mowing the lawn and cleaning up the yard, I shower and head to town. I start with my grandparents, who are surprised to see me twice in one day. Sunny and I play cards while Annie and Sis crochet. I get us pizza takeout from The Tavern, and we sit around and watch a baseball game.

Sunny and Sis go to bed, and I must fall asleep on the couch because I wake to my phone buzzing, and it's dark outside.

"Jenna," I groggily say. "Is everything okay?"

All I hear on the other end is heavy breathing.

"Jenna. Where are you?"

"Leaving," she mutters. "The Pool Hall."

I don't even take the time to get into my car. Instead, I jog the block and a half and am there approximately one and a half minutes after Jenna calls. She stands on the sidewalk, looking at her car. The passenger window is broken, and a brick is on the seat. There's a letter attached to it, and in big, black letters, it says, bitch.

My mind goes in a hundred directions. There could be fingerprints on the brick, but Eli is a cop, so I'm guessing he took care of that detail. I also don't want to leave the car here for everyone in town to see. Jenna would be humiliated by that kind of attention. This is a small town, and people talk.

"Give me your keys," I hold my hand out. "And get in the back."

We drive to Jenna's house, and I park the car in the garage then close and lock it.

"Jenna." I take her hand, and she fumbles with the keys. "Pack a bag. You're sleeping at the cottage tonight. We'll walk down to Sunny and Sis's and get my car. Yours is evidence."

Jenna heads to her room, and I look around her house. It's empty, much like my condo in Chicago. There are no pictures up or anything that shows Jenna's personality. She has a small round table in the kitchen and one couch in the living room. The place is sad and doesn't feel like her home. This is now my second time here, but the first time, I didn't notice the details of how little she had here. But now, it's all I can look at.

It only takes her a few minutes to put a few things in a bag, and we walk down Main Street to my car, and when we reach it, I drive Jenna out to the cottage. I make the bed in the guestroom, realizing we've barely spoken. I've been tied up in knots, and I forgot to pause and ask Jenna how she is.

"Jenna." She looks at me, standing across the room. "This is going to be the dumbest question I've ever asked you, but I'm going to ask it anyhow. Are you okay?"

She shakes her head and blots her eyes with her fingertips. "I don't think he's ever going to stop."

Jenna walks toward me, and I pull her into a hug. I cup her face in my hand. "Do you want to move back in with your parents? At least until you leave town."

Jenna shakes her head and takes a deep breath. "I love my parents, but it felt suffocating living there. My mom followed me around. Made sure I was in bed at a certain time. That I was taking my vitamins. She means so well, but I can't."

Her body shakes, and I know I have a small part of the story between her and Eli, but whatever has happened to her, and continues to happen, has a huge impact on her mental well-being. I close the two windows in the guest room and lock them so Jenna will feel extra safe, and then I walk to the door.

"Get some sleep, and let's talk this through in the morning."

Jenna nods, and I pause at the door, and look back at her. She wipes away another tear, and I can't get over how broken she looks. Her spirit, what makes Jenna a magnet to me, has all been zapped from her face.

"It's going to be okay," I say.

The look she gives me back says that she doesn't believe me.

Chapter Fifteen

Jenna

Two Years Ago

THAT YEAR'S LABOR DAY FIREWORKS were especially beautiful. I leaned back on my blanket and admired them. Or maybe it was because so many of us were gathered this year. Or, most importantly, it could be because Jake and Camilla seemed to have worked things out. They joined us, holding hands and were unable to keep their eyes off each other.

After the fireworks, the adults headed into the Bergland cottage where they were staying, and Robby and I walked down the gravel road. The cicadas were boisterous, and Robby used his phone as a flashlight, as big toads sometimes jumped in front of us. I screamed every time it happened.

"We deserve all the credit." Robby playfully pushed my arm. "Our siblings are grossly in love."

I smiled. "I think it's cute."

Robby made a vomiting sound. "Yeah, cute. That's one word for it."

We reached Jake's house, and like we'd done all summer, we headed into the guestroom closest to the entrance like we owned it—like sleeping here had become a right. And that sleeping in the same room together was also a given. We fell into this routine early in the summer, and every time Robby came to town, we fell right back into it.

Robby stretched his arms up into the air, and his shirt came up with it, and revealed smooth and muscular skin underneath.

"Okay, fine, it's cute," Robby said. "I've been worried about Camilla, well, her entire life. But Wheaton suits her. Your brother suits her."

I leaned in and whispered in Robby's ear. "You just don't want to think of your sister and my brother—"

"Don't say it." Robby put a finger over my lips, and I smiled against the pressure of the touch.

"Need to brush my teeth." Robby walked into the bathroom, where he now kept a spare toothbrush, and I looked around the room.

The extra mattress was in the closet, pushed up against the wall. I always pulled it out for Robby, assuming that was where he'd be most comfortable sleeping, but I didn't want to. I'd spent my entire life having platonic friendships with guys. I'd always gravitated toward male friendships, but how did I tell Robby that I didn't feel that way toward him? That I felt more. I'd spent the summer waiting and hoping he'd make a move, and he hadn't. Even though, at times, I felt the energy shift between us.

Robby returned to the room, now in shorts and a fitted shirt, and I tried not to stare. I went into the bathroom and looked at myself in the mirror. I'm not an unattractive person. Some would even call me pretty. I reached into the bottom cabinet drawer where I stashed some clothes, pulled out a pair of shorts, took my sweatshirt off, and went out in my tank top.

When I entered the room, Robby stood there, and I took it as a good sign that he didn't pull out the mattress. His eyes combed over my body. He stood against the wall, and we stared at each other. I put my hands on my hips, and Robby drug a hand across his face.

"Bed?" I pulled my lips into my mouth.

Robby nodded. "I could sleep."

Neither of us made a move. I considered getting into the bed, and then Robby could decide if he got in with me or went into the closet for the extra mattress. The only sound in the room was my heavy breathing.

A switch flipped in me, and I felt like I had an out-of-body experience. I'd never been forward, but I'd never felt this drawn to someone either. I closed the distance between us, reached up onto my toes, put my hand on the backside of his neck, and kissed him. On the lips. It was an innocent, probing kiss, and when I didn't feel it reciprocated, I ended it.

"Jenna." Robby's breath was labored. His chest heaved up and down.

The next move was his. Seconds passed, and his eyes darkened as he glanced at my lips. His arm reached out, wrapped around my waist, and he pulled me toward him until we were flush. His other hand reached around my neck, pressed his lips to mine, and turned me so I was pressed against the wall.

His lips parted mine, and his kisses were firm and needy. I imagined what type of kisser Robby would be more times than I'd like to admit, and I thought he'd kiss gentler. Soft, pleasant, and delicate. But there was nothing gentle about his touch. His mouth ravished mine, as if he'd wanted this as long as I have.

He took his hand, hooked it behind my knee, and pulled my leg up until it was wrapped around him. Robby pressed his erection against my core, and he was so rock hard I felt like I could lose my Robby-virginity card through both layers of our clothing.

But then he dropped my leg and took a step back. "I can't."

I breathed through my mouth, unable to catch my breath. Robby put his head in his hands. His breathing was as heavy as mine.

"Robby." I blinked rapidly, trying to find focus again. "What's wrong?"

"Fuck." Robby sat on the bed, head still in his hands. I leaned against the wall, not sure what happened. My legs felt like they were going to give out from underneath me. That kiss.

"Jenna," Robby said, finally looking at me. "I shouldn't have. We can't."

My tank top was bunched up, and I smoothed it out while studying Robby's face. I rubbed my lips together. My brain and mouth were out of sync, and I struggled to find words. I sat next to Robby at the foot of the bed.

"Jenna." Robby lifted his leg onto the bed, so he could better face me. A second passed. Then a few more, and my only companion was our heavy breaths and this thing between us. Our eyes met. "I have a girlfriend."

Blood drained from my face, and I looked at Robby, mouth open. From the very first day he visited Wheaton that summer, we'd spent every day talking for hours. Whether in person or even when he'd been home in Chicago, we'd had calls that have lasted for hours. The conversations were always appropriate, but in all of my friendships, I'd never spent that much time talking on the phone.

"How is it possible that in the hundred hours we've spoken this summer, you've never mentioned a girlfriend?" The words came out slowly and breathily.

"Lilly never came up—"

She had a name. I felt like I'd been punched in the stomach. Lilly. I stood and put my hands over my face. "I came to Chicago for a long weekend to look at schools. I stayed in your building. We talk on the phone for hours. You couldn't have mentioned a girlfriend at any point?"

Robby's mouth opened, but nothing came out. He stood up and ran his hand over his face. "I didn't think," he started to say, then continued, "Things are complicated back home. I didn't know how you felt. About me."

"You don't know how I feel?" I blew out an audible breath. "We talk for hours every day. Do you do this with all of your friends? Because I don't."

"Jenna." Robby walked to me but then turned and faced the wall. "No. I don't do this with everyone. I don't do this with anyone. Only you."

Clarity hit me like a ton of bricks. Everything became clear in my mind. "You strung me along until you figured out if you and your girlfriend, sorry, you and Lilly had a future together."

"Fuck, Jenna. No." Robby looked at me, his eyes were hooded, and he looked tired. "I'd never string you along. I would never hurt you. Never."

I laughed. "Where did you think this was headed?"

"I mean—" Robby began.

"Did you not think it would lead to this at some point? Was the chemistry only on my end?"

Robby stood in the corner of the room, perhaps a metaphor for how he was feeling. He shook his head. "Jenna, I have feelings—"

"Don't." I cut him off.

"But I'm not a cheater. I'd never cheat, and now we've kissed, and I had to stop it."

I laughed again. Not because this conversation was funny, but because I was uncomfortable, and it was heart-retching. And because of fucking Lilly.

"What would Lilly think if she knew we talked every day? That you send me a text the moment you wake up?"

"I know, Jenna. I know."

"What would she think if she knew that when you come to Wheaton, we stay in a room together? Every single time. Talking until the sun comes up. Telling each other all of our hopes and dreams."

"Jenna." Robby sat on the bed again and buried his head in his hands. "I know what'd she think."

"Then don't tell me that you're not a cheater because Lilly would not be okay with any of it. And now I look like a fool. For thinking the things I thought and for acting on it."

Robby stood up. He closed his eyes and rubbed his temples. "You're not the fool. I am."

"That's for damn sure."

Robby reached his hand out to me, but I backed up. "I don't want to lose you, Jenna."

My eyes began to swell with tears, and I blinked them back. I would not let him see me cry. "I don't think there is anything left to say to each other."

"Jenna." Robby put his hands on my shoulders, but I pushed them off.

"You need to go."

He paused, and his eyes pleaded with me. But after a moment, he turned, and walked out of the room.

Chapter Sixteen

Robby

JENNA IS STILL SLEEPING. I stepped out two hours ago to call Sunny and tell him I'd miss coffee with the men today, but I can't be gone when she wakes up. So instead, I've read the *New York Times*, *Wall Street Journal*, and *Wheaton Happenings* all before I hear her feet on the ground in the guest room.

She walks out of the room and doesn't see me at first. She stretches her arms high into the air and yawns, but no sound comes out. Looking at her still leaves me breathless. Forget the fact that she is a combination of my top ten celebrity crushes, all molded together, but her personality is everything.

I fold the *Wall Street Journal* over my lap, and Jenna's eyes dart in my direction.

"Sorry, Robby. I didn't see you there."

I smile. "How'd you sleep?"

"Better than I have in a while. I swear I don't always sleep until ten."

"There's coffee, or if you'd rather, you can make an espresso."

She raises an eyebrow. "Only you would have an espresso machine at a cottage."

"Well, you know," I tease. "I try to bring a bit of the city with me wherever I go."

Jenna rolls her eyes. "Well, thank you. I think I'll take you up on that espresso."

She pours herself a cup and holds it with both hands, and when it reaches her lips, she moans like it's the best thing she's ever had.

"Do you need to stop into the paper today? Or can we go right to the station?"

Jenna looks at me and bites her lip. "I've been thinking a lot about this, and it's not enough. They're going to minimize my concerns. I've seen it so many times."

"They won't, Jenna." I stand up and walk to where she leans against the counter in the kitchen. "Someone threw a brick through your window with the word bitch on it. Eli wrote you a letter saying he would get you back, no matter what. This isn't nothing."

Jenna closes her eyes but nods. "Can I use your shower? We can go after."

"Of course." I go into the bathroom and show her where the clean towels are. "No rush. We'll go after."

When I hear the shower sound, I scroll through my phone. Dax is one of my best friends, but I decide to call Jake first. No one messes with Jake. I'm not sure if it's his six foot, five-inch stature, that he played in the NFL, or that he doesn't mess around, but if I was going through something, that's the guy I'd want on my side. I told Jenna that I'd let her brothers know if anything else happened, and I wasn't joking around.

Jake answers on the first ring. "Is everything okay?" That's how people respond when they aren't used to getting a call from you.

"Jake," I say, taking the phone and walking outside. "I can't talk long, but there's something I need to tell you."

He doesn't say anything as I take a minute or two to go through everything Eli has put Jenna through the past few months. I tell him there is no proof that the brick was him but that we plan to go to the station and inquire about an order of protection.

"Mother fucker," Jake says when I'm done. "I never liked that guy. Gave me the absolute creeps. When will you get to town? I'm meeting you at the station."

I walk inside just as I hear the shower turn off. "Jake. Jenna is already uncomfortable. I don't think she's going to want an audience there."

"I'm her brother, Robby. Me. Not you. I should be there. And she needs to stay with us. I'm going to call some buddies and get her security."

"Jake," I whisper. "I don't think that is what Jenna wants. Let me go with her today."

"Why you?"

"She called me last night after the brick incident. Of everyone she could call, she called me."

Jake's breath is loud on the other end. "Shaun is a Wheaton cop. He and I are buddies. Can I call him? Get his thoughts on what we should do next?"

"After we fill you in. And in the meantime, call Dax. But Jake."

"What?"

"Jenna doesn't want this to blow out of proportion. You and Dax have the right to know, but you aren't going to help any legal process if all of your friends go after Eli."

"Understood."

Jenna walks out of the bathroom, and I say into the phone, "I'll call you later."

I don't wait for him to say anything before I hang up.

Jenna looks at me. "Who was that?"

"Jake." I pull my lips into a line.

"He knows now?" Jenna runs a brush through her wet hair.

"He does."

Jenna nods and walks into the guest room.

WE ARRIVE AT THE POLICE station, and I have more than ten missed calls from Dax. I have the letter Eli wrote to her, and the brick still lies in her car, safely in her garage. We get inside, and after asking to speak to someone, a detective I've never seen greets us.

"How can I help you today?"

Jenna looks at me. "We want to speak to you about filing a police report. And maybe even an order of protection."

The detective furrows his brow and looks at me and then at Jenna. "Let's go to my office."

Jenna and I follow him back, and he motions us to take a seat. The detective sits behind his desk. "I'm Rafferty. And who am I speaking to today?"

"I'm Jenna Abram. This is my friend," she looks at me, "Robby Bergland."

"What's going on?" The detective folds his hands.

Jenna looks at me again and bites her bottom lip. Doubt spreads over her face, and she looks like this is the last place she wants to be.

"I," she stammers and then finds her voice. "I was dating a man. He's from Rosso, Eli Harpser. We dated off and on for about nine months."

Rafferty hands her a bottle of water, and Jenna accepts. "I broke things off for good in, I don't know, January or February. And then Eli started showing up places. A lot of places. When I'm at work. At my brother's house celebrating a holiday. At the store. At my home. He's everywhere."

The detective takes some notes and then looks at Jenna. "And has Eli ever threatened you in any of these interactions?"

Jenna takes a deep breath and looks at me. "Well, not really, but—"

"He also wrote her this note," I interrupt. I've already taken photos of it, and I hand the original to the detective.

Rafferty glances at it and then puts it on his desk. "Back to my question. Has he threatened you?"

"I can't prove it." Jenna cracks her knuckles, looking at her lap the entire time. "But last night, I got out of work, and my window was broken out, and the brick in my car had a message on it."

I hand Rafferty the photos I took and printed earlier. He takes them and nods.

"Do you have proof that it was Eli?"

Jenna shakes her head. "No. But I don't have any enemies here that I know of. It felt targeted. I don't know," she says again into her lap.

The detective leans back and crosses one leg over the other. "What do you hope to accomplish today?"

My urge to protect Jenna bubbles to the surface. "There are cameras on Main Street. I want you to look at the footage, and Jenna will press charges for vandalism if we can pinpoint who did it. She also wants an order of protection against Eli."

Rafferty leans forward, puts his elbows on his desk, and rests his head in his hands. "Did Eli hurt you while you were in a relationship with him?"

Jenna rubs her eyes. "Well." She looks at me and then at the detective.

He leans forward. "Would you like your friend to leave so we can speak alone?"

"No." Jenna shakes her head.

Rafferty takes more notes, and everything I'm feeling comes to the surface. Eli hurt Jenna in some way. He fucking hurt her. I can see it written all over her face. I want to punch a hole in the wall. To scream while simultaneously pulling Jenna into a hug.

"Look," I say. "I know what Minnesota's anti-stalking laws are. Jenna has felt scared, threatened, oppressed, persecuted, and intimidated. All of those buckets fit. And I don't care two shits that Eli is a cop. His behavior is—"

"Wait." Rafferty interrupts me. "Eli is a cop?"

"In Rosso," Jenna says. "For the past decade."

He puts his pen down and nods. "Look, Jenna. Robby. We'll look into criminal charges here. But if you want an order of protection, you have to go to the courthouse, and the clerk there will provide you with paperwork to fill out. A judge will have to review it and then make a determination."

"And in the meantime?" I ask.

"Document, document, document." Rafferty purses his lips as he stares back at us from behind his desk.

I walk Jenna out and put my hand on the small of her back. I open my car door for her, trying to read her face. Is she frustrated? Angry? Scared? All of the above?

When we both get into the car, I look at her. "After the courthouse, what next?"

Jenna looks at me and shakes her head. I put my hand over hers. "I guess after you can take me home."

"Do you want to go home?" I drive toward the courthouse.

"Not really," Jenna says. "I'm not feeling the safest at the moment if I'm being honest."

After the short drive, I pull into the courthouse parking lot. "By now, your whole family probably knows. I'm sure they'll all welcome you with open arms, but you are very welcome at the cottage with me."

"Robby, it's too much." Jenna unbuckles her seatbelt.

"Your brothers work. Your dad works, and your mom will annoy you. I won't leave your side. It could be fun." I wink at her and get her first smile of the day.

"Rafferty acted like I was blowing things out of proportion."

She's not wrong, but I think detectives always act that way. "Don't minimize this, Jenna."

She nods. "If you're sure, Robby, I guess I'm bunking with you for a few nights."

Chapter Seventeen

Jenna

IT'S BEEN THREE NIGHTS SINCE I started sleeping at the cottage, and it is the coziest and most peaceful place I think I've ever stayed. Robby seems to like having me here too. We've settled into a routine. We drive to town in the morning and go to Sunny and Sis's. We visit for a few minutes until Annie shows up, and then Robby and I walk with Sunny down to the Main Street Café.

Afterward, I spend a few hours at the paper. And Robby either stays in town at Sunny and Sis's, takes them out to the cottage, or takes them for a ride around the lake. The past few evenings, we've sat on the couch and watched a movie on Robby's laptop.

If Robby lived in Wheaton, I don't think I'd ever have the strength to leave this place. I'm glad he doesn't, though, because I'm not staying.

"Jenna," Juan says, toast flying out of his mouth. "I don't understand why you'd want to leave Wheaton and move to a city. Cities are so suffocating."

Another day at the Main Street Café. Robby leans forward and rests his elbows on the table. "Small towns can feel suffocating too, Juan."

Juan makes a noise that resembles both a bark and a roar. "How so? We have all the room to spread out here and not run into people."

Robby doesn't back down, and I lean back in my chair, taking it all in. "It can feel suffocating to have everyone in a town know who you are, your parents, your siblings, and your business. In cities, I can disappear. There is great freedom in that."

I study Robby as he pulls up the collar of his obnoxiously blue and ironed polo shirt. Even in the middle of nowhere, Robby looks like he's been plucked from Wall Street and placed onto Main Street of Wheaton. Everything he wears is polished. When he decides to dress down, even his white sneakers have zero dirt on them. I have a theory that he irons his swim trunks too.

"You kids," Juan continues. "I'll never understand you."

Robby looks like he needs me to chime in as reinforcement. I turn to Juan. "Who knows? Maybe I'll come back here someday, but I've lived here almost my entire life, and there's an entire world out there I've never seen."

Sunny pats the top of my hand. "I love the adventure of you kids. It reminds me of our parents' generation. They left their countries behind for a better and different life."

"Exactly," Robby says. "And they never stopped feeling fondness for where they came from."

"Selfishly speaking." Walt grabs a toothpick from the center of the table and sticks it in his mouth. "I hate to see you go. We watch you kids grow up, and then poof, you're gone."

"Agreed." Lawson shakes his head. "Our town will die out at the rate we're going now."

"Precisely my point." Juan slams his hand down on

the table.

Watching Robby interact with these men, his grandma, and his niece scares me for all the feelings they've conjured up. He's ruined all other men for me, because I don't think anyone else can live up to him. He can hold a conversation, which already puts him in the top ten percent. He's funny, relatable, and nice to look at. I'm not even mad at him anymore.

After the café, we drop Sunny off at home, and Robby walks me to the paper. He holds the door open for me, and the air conditioning of the building makes my arms pebble in goosebumps.

"Will you come back to the cottage after work?"

Robby keeps the door open, and I turn to face him. "I'm working a double at The Pool Hall, so I won't be home until late."

He scratches his chin. "Any word from the detective? Or the judge?"

"Nothing." I shake my head. "Should be any day now."

Robby stuffs his hands into the pockets of his seersucker shorts. "Be careful, Jenna."

"Always." I say goodbye and head up to my floor.

My article is nearly complete, but I stay at the paper for longer to check in on my applications and to work on a special interest piece that I'm submitting to a few magazines for hopeful publication. I write under a pseudonym, and not even those closest to me know I was the writer for an article that went viral for the magazine *Harper's Bazaar*. I only write under my real name for *Wheaton Happenings*, and I didn't submit any of these articles as part of my application process to journalism schools. I hope my *Harper's Bazaar* piece will solidify my getting into at least one of the schools I applied to.

Before work at The Pool Hall, I stop at the post office to pick up my mail and then drop by my house to get clean clothes. The risk of Eli seems to be in the past. I haven't seen him for a few days, and it seems silly to be staying at the cottage with Robby. I push those feelings down, though. I like it out there. It's fun spending this much time with Robby. I park in front, and when I reach the door, there's a box with a note taped to it. I look around, and the neighborhood is silent, except for Mrs. Dvorak's barking dog next door. I'm too shaken up to open the package or envelope, so I hurry inside, throw a few things in a bag, and am out of the place in less than three minutes.

The regulars sidle up to the bar at The Pool Hall, and I stand behind the bar. When the day shift turns into the night shift, Gavin shows up. He's a college student who occasionally picks up shifts during the summer.

The phone behind the bar rings, and Gavin answers it. "Hello? Hello?"

He shakes his head. "Looks like your stalker's back, Jenna."

Stalker. Gavin has no idea what I've been going through, but the word is still jarring. This has been happening during all my shifts lately. The phone rings, and there's only heavy breathing on the other end.

The phone rings again, and I wave Gavin away. "Let me get it this time."

"Hello?" I say into the receiver.

Again, there's only heavy breathing on the other end. "Hello," I say louder this time, and still nothing.

"Look, asshole. If you don't stop calling here, I'll call the cops." I hang up, only for the phone to ring again, and I grab it and take it off the hook. It looks like no one will be placing to-go orders tonight.

At ten, only two people are left in the bar, so I release Gavin. I walk around, and gather glasses from our earlier rush, then run them through the dishwasher.

The bell chimes as the door opens, and Robby walks in. I go behind the bar and start making him a Manhattan, and he takes a seat. I reach for the box and letter I received earlier and hand them to Robby.

"I found this in front of my house. I don't have the nerve to open it. Will you?"

Robby shakes his head. "Damn, Jenna."

He takes the letter and reads the note; this time it's typed. I lean across the bar, cleaning up, wiping things down, and getting rid of today's condiments. Robby raises his eyebrows.

He looks at me. "It's fucked up. All of it."

My chest feels tight. "It's him again?"

Robby nods and takes his car keys to cut through the tape on the box. He studies it. "This doesn't make sense. It's an article." Robby turns it over and hands it to me.

It's not just an article. It's my article. The one I wrote and submitted for *Harper's Bazaar*. The one that got published and reposted by several A-list celebrities. I wrote it under a pseudonym. How could Eli know this? He couldn't trace the name Eleanor Jenna, my grandma's first name, followed by mine, back to me.

This isn't an article I put in the mail. I submitted it on my laptop directly to their site. I put my hands to my face as heat floods it. I shake my head repeatedly.

Robby reaches for my hand. "Jenna, what is it?"

"See you next time, Jenna." The final two customers walk out. I follow them and then lock the door.

"That's my article, Robby." I walk back to him. "I wrote that. How could he know? Unless he's monitoring my email. Can he do that? How would he do that? Is it spyware?"

"Wait." Robby scratches his facial hair in a downward motion. "You're Eleanor Jenna?"

"Focus, Robby."

He stares at me. His mouth falls open. "I read this article. Fuck, Jenna."

Robby walks around the bar and starts making me a drink. "Cosmo is still your favorite?"

I nod.

"Sit down. Let me serve you."

Robby hands me a Cosmo and then makes himself another drink. "The article isn't detailed enough for him to realize it's about him."

I blow out a breath. "Nor does Eli have the self-awareness ever to reach that conclusion."

"When we get back to the cottage, we need to change your passwords. On everything."

"And then we need to run a spyware check."

When my glass is empty, Robby hands me a new drink that he has already prepared. He would have made an excellent bartender. He pours himself another one too. Robby then comes around the bar and sits on the stool beside me, spinning until he faces me.

He holds his glass up to mine, and we clink them together. "Jennifer Aniston posted your article on her Instagram page. It got, like, five million likes."

I tuck my hair back. "You follow Jennifer Aniston?"

"Irrelevant, Jenna." Robby holds his glass to his lips and smiles. His eyes peer at me from above it. "You're famous."

"Eleanor Jenna is famous." I set my drink down and cross my legs. "Jenna Abram is just a small-town girl looking to move to the big city."

Robby shuts his eyes and inhales through his nose, and then his big, brown eyes are back on me. "Your article. He hurt you."

"Well, not physically," I quickly say. "I mean, not really."

There's so much I didn't put in the article.

"But Jenna." He stops talking and presses his lips into a line. "The things I want to do to him."

Robby's voice trails off.

It hits me that now that Robby knows this article is mine, he knows many of the intimate details of my abusive relationship with Eli. I've never told anyone these things, at least not with my real name. Now he knows, and I feel cut wide open.

He leans forward. "I need to say something to you, and if I don't say it tonight, I might never find the courage."

The human brain fascinates me. My imagination visits a million places while Robby contemplates his next words.

Chapter Eighteen

Robby

I'M THREE DRINKS IN, SO my mind is both a little fuzzy while simultaneously being really fucking clear. And without having this conversation, I can't move forward in this relationship with Jenna, whatever it is.

"That night two summers ago—"

"Oh, we're doing this." Jenna puts her head in her hands. "The night I kissed you."

"No, Jenna." I put my hand on her shoulder, and when she moves her hands from her face, it's red. "Your kiss was innocent. Mine wasn't."

Jenna takes a long sip of her drink. "My kiss wasn't that innocent."

My mind flashes to that night. I've thought about it every day since it happened. Like I'm floating above and watching the two of us. If it had been in slow motion, I would have had time to do things differently. I remember looking at Jenna, and wanting to tell her about Lilly, so there would be no lies between us, and then she kissed me. And there was nothing in the world that could have prevented me from kissing her back. To this day, I'm still not sure how I was able to stop.

It was the best kiss of my life.

"You were right about everything. I purposely hid Lilly from you."

Jenna stands up, walks around the bar, and pours a beer from the tap. She removes the foam from the top of the glass. "Why not tell me? How hard would it have been?"

I look down at my hands. Only the truth will do. And for the past two years, I've longed for a moment where I could tell her everything.

"If I had told you about her, you never would have allowed yourself to get close to me."

Jenna barks a laugh. "And that would have saved me a lot of heartache."

She takes her beer and sits by me once again.

"My relationship with Lilly was terrible. I know that's cliché, but I'd wanted to end things for a while. So had she, as it turns out. And talking to you about your ex-fiancé, and getting out, and being strong, I was trying to draw strength from you."

Jenna's eyes penetrate mine, and I can almost see her brain spinning at the information I spew out.

"When I got back to Chicago after the July fourth holiday two summers ago, I was going to end things with her." I stir the straw in my drink. "When I got home, she told me her grandma died, and I couldn't be the ass who breaks up with a girl after a death in her family."

Jenna crosses her legs, and I continue. "Lilly ended up going home to Michigan for the funeral and worked remotely from there for almost the entirety of that summer."

Jenna continues to stare at me. She's studying my face and every word. "I had feelings too. What I did was unfair, and it led you on even though I wanted to be with you more than anything. And I was too big of a coward to end things with Lilly earlier so you and I could start something, the right way."

The words fall out of my mouth in one long and broken sentence.

Jenna turns her head to the side, examining me. "And where are things at with Lilly now?"

"We broke up. The day I went back to Chicago after Labor Day weekend. The week after, she was dating a guy I once considered a close friend."

Jenna holds her beer to her lips and takes a long sip. "Were you honest with her about everything?"

"Yes." Jenna raises her eyebrow. "I told her all about you. Admitted to an emotional affair. Told her about our kiss. Everything. The crazy thing is that Lilly didn't even seem to care. We spent six years together, and it was probably five years too long."

Jenna leans down and rests her head in her hand. "I assumed she was in London with you that entire time."

"She was." I look outside, thinking I see something from the corner of my eye. "Lilly was there with her now fiancé and my former friend, who also works for Goldman Sachs."

I continue. "I called and texted several times."

"Yeah," Jenna looks down. "I blocked your number, and then I had my number changed, you know, because of the stalker situation."

She looks up and bites her bottom lip. "I had feelings for you, you know? Of course, you know. And even though you weren't mine, I felt cheated on too."

My stomach lurches, and I feel a heaviness in my chest. "How? Why?"

"Because you'd spend time with me, then go to

Chicago and spend time with her. I mean, of course, right? She was your girlfriend."

"It was mutual. The feelings between us." The words vomit out of me. I put my hand on her arm. "And I wasn't going home and sleeping with Lilly. When I say things were strained, I'm being honest. I'm not saying it for your benefit or for me to look better. I know I behaved poorly, but my relationship with Lilly was practically non-existent the summer I spent hanging out with you."

Feelings bubble up in my chest. I'm relieved I'm finally telling her this and scared over how much I admit. "Jenna, from that very first day when we climbed the water tower, I've been yours."

Jenna's face changes. She pulls her lips into a line, and then shakes her head and rubs the bridge of her nose. "Why are you telling me this? Why now? I'm moving. You're moving. Our lives are on completely different paths."

"Jenna, why didn't you let me explain all of this after it happened? Why did you ghost me like that?"

Jenna closes her eyes and rubs her lips together. "I knew if I heard you out, you'd explain things so I couldn't stay mad at you."

I raise my eyebrows. "And that's a bad thing?"

"Because of everything I said earlier, yes, it's a bad thing." Jenna leans on her hand. "You were in Chicago. I was in Wheaton. I'm headed somewhere for school. You're going to be somewhere else for a new career path."

"Jenna," I say her name slowly. "We just admitted that we felt the same way about each other."

"Yes." Jenna looks at me. "And now we know. But it doesn't change anything."

To me, it changes everything. It's rare to feel this level of magnetism with someone. And it's even more uncommon when two people feel the same way. It's not nothing.

We both turn to the window when something goes barreling through it. My first instinct is to pull Jenna down to the ground and protect her from the shards of glass.

"Jenna, call the police," I say, panting, and pulls out her cell phone.

When the threat seems over, I walk over to the broken window to see a brick lying on the ground. A note attached reads, "Watch your back, whore."

Chapter Nineteen

Jenna

IT'S AFTER TWO IN THE morning when my head hits the pillow at the Bergland cottage. After the cops showed up and took our statements, the bar owner Dave arrived and had to board up the window for the night. I knew I saw something out of the corner of my eye, and my skin crawls. Someone could have been watching us from the floor-to-ceiling windows.

After that, and my conversation with Robby, I have little hope for sleep tonight. We felt the same way about each other, and I should feel relief, but instead, I feel changed. By everything that's happened in my life since that magical summer. Although I thought I was dying to hear those words from him, once he said them, it became clear that whatever is happening between us can only be temporary.

At some point, I must doze off, because when I open my eyes the sun peeks through the windows, and I glance at my phone. It's almost noon. I hear a clanking noise from the kitchen. I run a brush through my hair and go to investigate the noise.

Robby stands at the stove, and I lean against the wall

and smile as he flips a pancake, and then pours more batter on the pan.

"Good morning," I say. There are pans everywhere, and pancake mix all over the countertops.

Robby turns to me and smiles. "Good morning to you."

I walk to the fridge and grab orange juice and pour us both a glass. "Are you making me pancakes, Robby Bergland?"

He grins, and then flips another pancake onto a plate, that is already very full of pancakes.

"I can make about three things really well. And pancakes are one of those things."

"We'll see about that." I grab a plate from the counter, and put some of the pancakes on it, and walk to the table. Robby follows.

"How long have you been up?" I ask him, pouring syrup on my plate.

"Hours," he says, taking a seat across from me. "I can't sleep in. It's both a blessing, and a curse."

With my fork, I cut into a pancake, dip it in the syrup, and take my first bite. And I groan. I can't help it. It's that good.

"Robby," I say slowly, drawing out every syllable in his name. "What did you do to these?"

He laughs. "Not bad, right?" Robby watches me as I take another bite. I close my eyes and lick the syrup off of my lips. I didn't even think I was hungry, but it turns out, I was completely ravenous.

"Not bad?" I lift an eyebrow. "These may be the best things I've ever had."

Robby takes a break from staring at me, to eat his own pancakes. "Can you play hooky from the paper today? I want to take you to a festival nearby."

My eyes dart to his. "A festival. What festival?"

"Gracetown is having their first annual grape stomping festival. I thought we could go."

"How do you know about the festival in Gracetown?" I stifle a laugh. "I've never been, but Robby from Chicago is aware of its existence."

"Okay." Robby claps his hands together. "After you're done eating, you can shower, and then we're headed to Gracetown. And wear something that can get messy."

After my shower, Robby drives me about thirty miles away to Gracetown. I haven't been to this town since I was a child, and don't remember much about it. It's situated on a lake, and once we park, I can see tents set up selling merchandise, food, and activities. But now that there's a winery here, I'm sure a lot more people will visit.

Robby jogs to my side of the car and opens the door for me.

"I read about this festival in the paper," Robby says. "It sounded really fun."

We walk along the lake front, stopping at different shops that catch our eyes. When I see cheese samples, I grab Robby's arm, and pull him into the shade of the tent.

"I'm obsessed with cheese," I say to no one in particular, but the lady behind the table laughs.

"Then you have to try this one." She puts a couple of slices on a small plate and then spoons a fig spread next to it. "It's called Friesago, and it's made from sheep's milk."

I moan as I bite into the firm cheese. Robby takes a slice, and his eyes roll into his head, and then he licks his lips.

"This is a great cheese," the lady continues. "The aromas are really mild. And I find the flavors nutty, milky, grassy, tangy, and piquant."

Robby leans toward me and speaks into my ear. "Yes. Exactly what she said."

A chuckle escapes me, and I take another slice. "This is honestly some of the best cheese I've ever had."

"You heard the lady," Robby winks at me. "We will take some of this." He then points at another cheese. "And I'd love to get that brie as well."

The lady packages it up, and we work our way to the grape stomping area. Robby holds the bag of cheese.

"Watching your face when you ate that cheese," Robby says. "Was like getting to know you for the first time."

"What can I say?" I shrug my shoulders and smile at him. "I really love cheese."

We arrive at the large barrels of grapes. Robby nods toward an empty barrel. "What do you think, Jenna? Should we try it?"

I hesitate, but Robby's excited face convinces me. "Okay, let's do it."

We remove our shoes, and Robby holds my hand as I step over the barrel and into the grapes. They squish between my toes, and it feels oddly satisfying.

"It's so gross." Robby laughs, putting his hands on my shoulders for balance. "But it's also—"

"Totally amazing," I quickly say.

"Yes, exactly."

We laugh as we stomp on the grapes, watching our barrel turn to more liquid, and less solid. I don't know if it's the texture, or that I'm stomping on these grapes, but the entire thing feels therapeutic.

"You haven't lived until you've stomped grapes." Robby smiles at me and looks so boyishly happy.

When there is nothing left in the barrel to stomp, Robby gets out first, and holds his hand out to me. We both slip and Robby goes down first, but I quickly follow, until we're lying in the grass, covered in red grapes. I land on top of Robby, and our chests heave against each other from our laughter, and I push off of him.

Robby sits up, and wipes grass off of his shorts. "I guess we underestimated how slippery grapes are."

"Yeah," I say, standing up, and hold my hands out to help Robby up. "I guess so."

"There's a spigot." Robby points. "Let's wash our feet off."

We walk to the fountain of water, holding on to each other, trying to stay upright. When we reach the spigot, we both plop down. Robby takes my slimy feet in his hands, and runs them under the water, while squeezing my arches, and then spreads my toes, threading his fingers through them, and letting the water clean me everywhere.

"Here," I say. "Let me do yours."

I pull Robby's legs onto my lap, and watch as the purplish-red liquid runs off his feet, and onto the grass. I move his pinky toe out of the way, letting the water trickle in all the crevasses. I bring the hose up his leg, wash his calves, and run my hands down his muscular leg. I'm totally lost in the sensation of washing Robby, and when my head jerks up, I'm suddenly aware that I'm cleaning parts of him that aren't grape stained, Robby stares at me.

The corners of his mouth turn up slightly in a smile, and he doesn't say anything. When I became aware that I'm still gripping his leg, I release.

"All better." I reach up and turn off the water.

Robby stands up and puts his hands out and helps me get to my feet.

"Today's been fun," I say, and Robby's gaze moves down my face, until it settles on my lips.

"And it's not even over yet."

The rest of the day is easy, like every moment with Robby is. Effortlessly easy. There is never a shortage of things to discuss, or an opportunity to hope for a smile, because Robby smiles and laughs so easily. He acts like everything I say is cute and funny. Like I matter.

"What do you say we head back to the cottage and tear into all the cheese we bought today?" Robby points down at the now two bags of cheese in his hands.

"Yes," I say, clapping my hands together. "But then we should pick up some crackers. Maybe salami and olives. We could make a charcuterie board."

The words excitedly come out of my mouth, and Robby laughs. He nudges my shoulder and studies me.

"Serious question, Jenna." Robby opens the car door for me and places the bags in the backseat. "If you could live on either cheese or my pancakes for the rest of your life, what would you choose?"

Robby shuts my door and runs around the car to the driver's side. He gets in the car and looks at me.

"You can't make me choose," I say. "They both fulfill such different cravings, you know?"

Robby backs the car out of our parking spot, and without looking at me, says, "I'm pretty sure I could live the rest of my life happy by only watching you enjoy food."

"Well." I lean toward the middle console. "You said you make three things, so if you ever want to make me whatever those other two are, I will gladly make you happy."

We ride most of the way to the cottage in silence. I haven't let myself fixate on all the things I missed about spending time with Robby, but now that I'm with him, I let myself revel in how good it feels to have this important relationship back in my life. It feels like there's an end date on it, but I vow to enjoy the time I have with him.

Chapter Twenty

Robby

$\mathcal{H}$AVING JENNA STAY AT THE cottage is the best thing ever, even if it is because she's got a stalker ex-boyfriend. We spend the days together, and talk so late into the evenings, that last night, I had to bring Jenna to bed after she fell asleep on the couch. I'm so happy to have her back in my life. Not only as my friend, but my best friend. I hadn't realized how big of a void there was not having her to talk to.

Today I promised I'd make Jenna my famous BLT. It's one of the three things I make really well, and the trick is that I use my homemade mayonnaise.

"It smells amazing in here." Jenna walks out of the guestroom, hair still wet from showering. "I can't believe in all the time I've known you I'm only now getting to eat these three amazing meals."

Jenna stands next to me at the counter, and I glance at her. Beads of water run down her forehead, and she takes her hand and wipes them away. "Takeout is easier."

"Yeah," Jenna says, licking her lips. "But it's kind of sexy that you cook. Even if it is only three things."

A laugh barks out of me, and Jenna continues. "Women like that sort of thing. You should lead with it."

I slather mayonnaise on the bread and put it on the pan to warm it up. "At this rate, I'm thinking celibacy may be my thing."

Jenna shakes her head, and I regret saying it as soon as it comes out of my mouth. "Robby. I highly doubt celibacy is in your future. I mean, look at you." Jenna gestures her hand toward me.

The air in the room grows thick. I put the crispy bacon, lettuce, and tomato on the toasted bread and put it on a plate for her. I then make myself one, and we sit at the table.

My eyes stay on Jenna, because I'll know how she feels the moment she bites into her sandwich. One of my favorite things about Jenna is her inability to hide how she's feeling. Her emotions are worn all over her face and body language.

"Holy shit," Jenna says. She closes her eyes, chews, and then opens them. A dollop of mayonnaise is on the corner of her mouth, and she jets her tongue out to get it. "Incredible. To die for. I could live on this, and your pancakes, for the rest of my life."

"And cheese," I interrupt.

Jenna's mouth turns up in a smile. "Of course, cheese. And this third mystery thing you cook."

Jenna takes another bite, and the enjoyment is all over her body. I don't even bite into my BLT because I enjoy watching her too much.

"How can someone that makes the world best pancakes and BLT, not cook other things?"

When Jenna finishes, I stand up, and usher us out the door, because today we've decided to go on a hike. We walk side by side, and I turn to her.

"I didn't say I don't know how to cook anything else. Only that I don't cook anything else. It's easier to order takeout, or buy prepackaged salads, and things like that."

We cross the road and start on the trail that leads up into the hills, and Jenna bends down and grabs a stick on the ground. "Will I get to try this mysterious third meal you're good at?"

"Maybe," I say slowly. "But then I'll be out of tricks up my sleeve. How will I keep you interested?"

Jenna bits the corner of her bottom lip. "Oh Robby. Why do I have a feeling that you have so many tricks up your sleeve that a girl could get dizzy from them?"

We always end up in this same spot, Jenna and me. We're friends who can talk about the real and serious stuff, but there is always this flirtatious nature to it. I have many female friends, and it doesn't exist there. Something is different when it comes to us. And these feelings are always right below the surface, and although I know that Jenna feels strongly about leaving and never looking back, I can't help but feel the inevitable pull that we're meant to be more than friends. More than best friends.

***

AFTER OUR LONG HIKE, AND showers, we settled in and watched some murder mystery on Netflix, before saying goodnight around midnight. But now, I lie awake in bed, with way too many thoughts for sleep to come. It doesn't even feel close.

Lightning flashes in through the windows, and I finally give up and walk out to the kitchen.

"Jenna." Her presence surprises me. She leans against the counter in nothing but a crop top t-shirt and shorts that are much too short. My breath hitches in my throat.

"I'm sorry." Jenna sticks a fork into the Tupperware

she holds, stabs a piece of pineapple, and puts it in her mouth. "Did I wake you? I was trying to be quiet."

"Ah, no." I shake my head and comb my fingers through my hair. "I didn't hear anything. I came looking for a late-night snack."

"The lightning woke me." Jenna nods toward the open window. "Look at it. The sky seems angry tonight."

The light pulsates the sky, illuminating both the lake and the hills.

Jenna stabs another piece of pineapple and holds the fork out to me. I walk over to her, open my mouth, and she feeds me.

"This is to die for." Jennifer moans as she takes a bite and then gives me another one. "Where did you get this pineapple?"

A ceiling fan hums over our heads, and although I can feel the breeze from it, I mostly only feel the warmth standing this close to Jenna. And the damn noises she makes when she likes food.

She points the fork at me, and her eyes leave mine, and roam down my body. "Can those even be considered shorts?"

I glance down, suddenly aware at how little I'm wearing.

"It's hot in here," I say. "I was hot."

Our eyes meet, and there's so much heat between us. I take slow breaths. Jenna takes the last bite of pineapple, and I grab the Tupperware out of her hand and put it on the counter.

"You've been working out." Jenna's eyes start at my collarbone but rake down my body. Her tongue darts out and wets her lips. When our eyes meet again, she shakes her head as if her previous lack of subtlety was subconsciously done.

"Are you checking me out?" I say, and Jenna's face flushes.

"I'm sorry." She starts fanning her face with her hand. "I didn't mean to—"

"It doesn't bother me," I say quickly. "You can check me out."

My eyes take in her body. "Because I'm definitely checking you out."

Jenna's chest expands as she takes a long breath in, and then slowly breathes out of her mouth. My hand squeezes her waist. Her skin is warm, her crop top not reaching this exact point. And then I take my other hand, and place it on the back of her neck, and I kiss her. The way she first kissed me. Gentle. Soft. Probing. When our lips touch, she lets out a noise, almost too quiet to hear. And then I pull away.

Jenna gives me a sideways smile like she knows what I'm doing and remembers our first kiss two years ago. She doesn't kiss me, though. Instead, she places her palms on my chest, spreads her fingers, and combs them down my bare chest. A breath hitches in my chest, and I hold it in. Her hands are cool against my warm skin, and I let out a whimper. The sound is foreign coming out of my mouth, but I can't help myself. Her touch feels like a long time coming.

Jenna reaches the waist of my shorts that hang low and hooks her thumbs underneath the fabric, not too deep, and then when she gets to my back, she spreads her fingers again. When our eyes meet, her mouth is slightly open, and I don't think she's testing me after all. She's going slow too and taking me in.

Her hands move to my shoulders, and she lets out a moan, and then her hands wrap around the back of my neck, she lifts herself onto her toes, and presses her lips against mine.

I lift Jenna onto the edge of the counter and push myself into her, and the pressure of my erection against her sends electricity pulsating through me. I reach for the hairband that holds her hair up on top of her head, and her long locks fall loose. She squeezes the back of my neck, pulling me closer, but our bodies are already pressed against each other as far as they'll go.

Her mouth is sweet from the fruit we shared, and her lips are hungry. She moves her hands to my ass, and I groan as she pulls me closer.

"Jenna," I speak into her mouth, not wanting to remove my mouth from hers, even for a moment. "Do you want this?"

"Yes," she breathily says into my mouth. I need Jenna to be comfortable. If we go any further, I need to be damn sure this is what she wants.

I pull away from her for a moment to ask, "Are we going too fast?"

I've wanted this for so long. I want everything to be perfect. And the deeper we go into this thing, the harder it will be to stop it from happening.

Jenna puts her hands on my face and speaks into our kiss. "From my calculations, we're two years late."

I laugh and lift Jenna, her legs wrap tightly around my waist, and I walk her to the bedroom.

Chapter Twenty-One

Jenna

ROBBY LAYS ME GENTLY ONTO his bed, and my legs stay wrapped around him the entire time. My back presses against his soft comforter, and I run my hands up his shoulders and scratch his dark facial hair. It's not thick enough to be considered an actual beard, and it's not something he had before this visit, and I can't get enough of it.

His hands stretch around my waist and slip under my sleep shirt until he grips both of my breasts. He slides the shirt over my head and kisses them like they're the best he ever felt. Robby's erection feels heavy against my stomach, then slides down my body until it's against my core.

Our kisses are frantic. Like, if we don't hurry this along, something might ruin the moment, and we'll be stuck waiting another two years, only imagining what it would feel like to be together. I can't let that happen. I grab his shorts and pull them down.

"Jenna." Robby pants, and his lips press into my neck. "Slow down."

He presses his forehead into mine, lifts his face, and

meets my eyes. His pinkies circle my skin, just under my shorts, and he moves to his knees to remove them. Robby stands up, lit by the lightning outside, and pulls his shorts the rest of the way down. I sit up, prop myself on my elbows, and take all of Robby in. Then I grab his arm and pull him onto me.

Robby combs his hand up my hip, then side and circles my nipples with his thumbs. I reach down and take him in my hand, and he lets out a cry.

"Fuck, Jenna." Robby rests his chin between my breasts and glances at me, breathing heavily. "I need." He blows out a breath. "Condom."

I pull his face to mine, part his lips, and kiss him deeply. He tastes incredible. Pineapple. I wrap one hand in his dark hair and scrape his back with my fingernails with the other. He rolls over my core.

"Jenna," Robby says again, this time more labored.

"No condom," I say into his mouth and lean forward, kissing his chest. "I'm clean. And on the pill." I struggle to form words. My mind is foggy from the anticipation.

Robby holds the back of my head as he pushes into me. Teasing at first, and then with one final thrust, I have all of him. I raise my eyebrows and hold my breath. I'm full. Completely and utterly filled with all of Robby. He hooks his hand behind my knee, and his other hand cups my face, and he glides over me.

He holds my gaze and looks at me like I'm the most precious thing in his universe. I brush hair out of his face, and reach up to kiss his eye, and then his other eye. Every nerve ending in my body is awakened by his fingertips across my face, the way his hand brushes down my arm, and the weight of his warm body on mine.

"This won't last long, I'm afraid." He puts his thumb between where our bodies meet and circles. "You feel too good."

The sensation of Robby thrusting in and out of me and whatever magic he's doing with that finger makes my body feel on the precipice of an explosion. His body is heavy, warm, and hard. There are no soft corners on Robby. Every part of him is an intricately designed angle. I need something to grab onto, to help me through this, so I grab his hair and pull.

"Jen—" Robby begins to say. "You're making me lose my mind."

My body fills with pleasure like I've never felt in my life. It's so consuming that my toes curl, and when it ends, I can't kiss, can't roll my hips, and can't articulate a thought. It doesn't matter because Robby is soon behind me. He groans into my neck, and it's not something delicate. It's carnal, masculine, and then all his weight is on me. His heart beats fast against mine.

Robby rolls off me, and we both lie on our backs, arms pressed against each other, staring at the ceiling. I've spent my adult life being disappointed in people for one reason or another. Maybe disappointed isn't the right word, but people generally have fallen short of my expectations. Robby knows how to touch a woman, and it's the least surprising thing I've ever discovered.

It's something I often thought about, and it was more than I imagined or hoped. Robby turns onto his side and rests his head on his arm. I move to my side as well. He presses his lips into mine and pushes my hair away from my face.

"Jenna." Robby takes my hand in his and places it on his heart. It's begun to slow down. "I won't be a truly happy man until we can do this about three million more times."

We smile. I want to respond, but my mind is jumbled. I'm at a crossroads between wanting to do that for the rest of my life and moving forward with my plan of leaving, knowing I can die happy because I experienced that level of connectivity once in my life, which is probably more than most people will ever be able to say.

Robby looks at me sheepishly, and his always perfect hair is tousled, and I take my fingers and run them through it.

"It wasn't my best performance." Robby strokes my arm and then grins. "In my defense, it's been a very long time. And you're quite sexy."

Robby pulls me in tighter, and my breasts push up against his chest.

"How long?" I rub his back. And once again, curiosity forces the question from my mouth.

Robby's lips go into a straight line. "You know how I told you I never slept with Lilly the summer we hung out two years ago?"

I nod. "Yeah."

"Well, before that." I study Robby's face for any signs of sarcasm, but he looks straight at me.

"Sorry. Are you saying you haven't had sex in over two years? But you were in London. With all those European women."

He chuckles, and his hand holds my face. He kisses my neck and then whispers into my ear. "I've never had casual sex. It's not my thing."

My hand moves from his back to his side, then down his leg. Everything about Robby is so masculine, and I love feeling every muscle. I've spent years admiring him but having access to him is much better.

"Plus, Jenna," Robby says my name slowly. He presses his open palm onto my breasts, pulling them together. "After that first kiss with you, I knew you'd ruined me for every other woman."

"I'm happy you broke your dry spell with me." I look down at his hand as he threads his fingers through mine.

"And I needed you to be the person…"

My voice trails off, and Robby presses his thumb into the bottom of my chin and lifts my head so I can meet his gaze. "You can talk to me."

His soft lips press into my forehead, and that small gesture gives me strength.

"Well, after him," I begin, not wanting to pollute this perfect moment with his name. "I wasn't sure if I'd ever feel safe doing this again."

Robby nods his head, takes a long blink, and I continue, "But you're you." Something catches in my chest at my words, but I push the feeling down.

"You make me feel safe. You are all goodness. This," I point to him, and then push my index finger into my chest. "Is what it's supposed to be like. But I was in something bad, for far too long, and I had forgotten. Until now."

Robby takes my hand and kisses it. "I would never hurt you. Ever Jenna. I'd never ask you to do something you weren't comfortable with. Take advantage of you. Ever."

"I know. That's what I'm telling you," I say.

Robby squeezes my hand tight in his.

"And for some reason, ever since all of that happened with him, I hoped for this. With you. Because you are everything." I trace my finger along his arms as I say these words.

"Jenna—" Robby begins to say, but I cut him off.

"And now I can leave," I say. "I can move away for school and not look back. You reminded me that there is goodness out there, and I won't feel the need to fixate on the bad. Because of you, I'll be able to start over somewhere new. You've breathed light back into me. Reminded me that it exists."

Robby studies me, with hooded eyes, and pursed lips. His mouth opens, like he's going to say something, but instead, he kisses my hand once again.

"I'll be here for you in any capacity you want me to be," he finally says.

"You're the epitome of goodness," I say into our kiss. "And no matter where life takes us, you'll always be one of my favorite people."

Robby's full lips find mine. Our kiss starts slowly, but then it deepens. He presses onto my back, holding us together. I feel him grow against me, just from kissing. This kiss is a lot different from our earlier one. It's smooth, buttery, and full of intention. It's also intimate like he only kisses this slowly for me. There's no rush this time, and his soft lips and tongue brushing against mine awaken every fiber of my being. He takes my leg and pulls it over him.

"If I only get you for a short time," Robby says, sprinkling my face with kisses. "I want to go slow."

His hips roll into mine, and he reaches his hand down, and once again, I'm full and speechless.

There was no sleep to be had until dawn, so I'm not surprised that the clock on the nightstand says noon when I do finally open my eyes. I roll over, expecting to feel Robby next to me, but he's not. I stretch my arms high into the air and take in the state of the room. My shirt is on the floor near the window, and my shorts are in a bunch by the door. Robby's shorts are in a corner, and on the nightstand are unopened condoms. Then I look down at myself. I'm naked, and my breasts and stomach are full of hickeys. Actual hickeys.

I peek out of the room, and there is still no sign of Robby. I pull last night's clothes on, and then search for my phone. I see it on the nightstand, grab it, and have several text messages from Robby. He wanted to let me sleep. He had to go to town for a meeting with an assisted living place. And then, he had a phone interview with Teaching America. He'll see me later.

As I step into the shower, my mind replays the events from last night. It felt like an inevitable gravitational pull between two people. I don't think anything could have stopped it from happening.

It's strange how everything and nothing changes at the same time. Last night somehow managed to change everything. What I will expect in future relationships, and what safe feels like. It also changes nothing. I know who I am, and I'm finally going to move forward with what I want next, and I'll always have love for Robby, but he doesn't fit into my plan.

I've never spent an entire evening making love on repeat. After our first frantic go, it changed into something entirely different. And it somehow only got better and more intimate. Last night felt like the start of a very long goodbye. When I get my call, I'm leaving, and I'll never change course because of a relationship. I've been stuck for too many years., I've been depressed, and unable to move on to the next thing, but I'm done.

When I get out of the shower, I glance at my phone and see a missed call. I listen, and it's a judge who reviewed my order of protection request. I call the number back.

"Yes, can you connect me with Judge Shuster?" I say to the woman who picks up.

"One moment, please."

Hold music plays, and I don't need to wait long before I'm connected.

"Judge Shuster speaking. And who is this?"

"Yes. Judge Shuster. This is Jenna Abram. I missed your call. I filed an—"

"Yes, yes." He cuts me off. "I reviewed your file, and there isn't enough evidence against Eli Harpser to grant you an order of protection at this time."

"Excuse me. But the man is stalking me. As I closed down The Pool Hall, a brick was thrown through the window. A package was left—"

"Ms. Abram." His heavy breathing is audible. "There is no proof that either brick incidents were Mr. Harpser."

"But—" I begin to say and am again cut off.

"My advice is to give him a chance to explain things. I made it a point to talk to his police colleagues in Rosso, and everyone thinks the world of him."

I end the call without saying goodbye, and it feels like the walls are caving around me. Is this our judicial system? Who is protecting me?

My heart tries to escape my chest as it beats heavily. I walk up the long driveway because I'm stuck here without a car, but luck is on my side today. My favorite local farmer, Ed, happens to be driving by and offers to give me a ride in. Even though my situation feels helpless, I still need to work and live. I sit at my desk at the paper and quickly glance over the article due tomorrow. It's good, almost ninety-five percent finished, and although I should work on it, I bring up a new word document and start writing a follow-up to the first article I had published in *Harper's Bazaar*.

After missing a few calls from Robby, my mom, then Camilla, I turn my phone off. Anyone who writes knows you have to strike while the iron's hot; today, the words are pouring out of me. My rage, helplessness, and disbelief all flow onto the paper. I name Eli. What's going to happen? Am I going to get sued for slander? He has no argument because everything I say is true.

I read through my article several times. I edit, make my words more concise, and then draft an email to the editor in chief, to whom I sent my last article that barely touched the surface of relationship abuse. This time, I introduce myself.

"Let me introduce myself properly," I write. "I'm Eleanor Jenna, but those who know me, call me Jenna Abram. Why did I write under a pseudonym? Because I was scared. Both of my tormentor and of being revictimized by public opinion. I'm not scared anymore. I am a survivor. This is my story."

I hover over save draft and send. I've never been spontaneous. I think everything through, and outing myself as Eleanor Jenna has ramifications for my family and me. Then I go for it and send the article to *Harper's Bazaar*.

Chapter Twenty-Two

Robby

WHEN JENNA WALKS THROUGH THE door to the cottage, I practically tackle her in relief. I called Jake and Dax hours ago, and the three of us were waiting while Camilla and Carrie drove around town looking for her.

Before I can speak, Jake stands up and puts his hands on his hips. "Where the hell have you been?"

Jenna looks at me, then Jake, and finally Dax, who crosses his arms and seems both pissed and concerned.

"I was at work. At the paper."

Dax stands up. "Why was your car at home then?"

"Jenna," I breathe her name out slowly. "We've been worried sick. I couldn't get ahold of you and saw your car at your house. I called Jake and Dax."

Her eyes cut to both of them. "Yeah, I see that."

"Jenna," Jake says more forcefully. "With everything going on, you can't do this to us."

"I'm sorry." She shakes her head. "I wasn't trying to worry you. I went to the paper, and I started writing and got distracted. I didn't charge my phone last night, and it died."

Jenna looks at me. Of course, she didn't charge her phone last night. She was having marathon sex with me.

"Have you heard from the judge?" Jake asks, gripping Jenna's arms.

"No. Soon, I hope." Something changes in her body when she says it.

I'm sure Jenna feels like she's suffocating right now, but I hope she knows that our concern is directly related to the amount she's loved.

Jenna slings her bag onto the couch. "Look. You both have kids. And women who are probably waiting at home for you, wishing you were there. I'm good."

Jake and Dax look at each other, and Jake shakes his head. Jenna has her older brothers wrapped around her finger. It was like this, even when we were all younger. There's something magnetizing and convincing in Jenna. To be around her is to know you're surrounded with something special. I can't help but smile. Fucking Jenna.

"You're lucky we didn't call Mom and Dad," Dax says on his way out.

Jenna rolls her eyes at the threat of a call to her parents, but she hugs Jake and Dax as they leave. When I hear the sound of their tires crunching against the gravel road, I rush to Jenna and sweep her into a hug. She pulls away, shaking her head.

"You called my brothers?" Her tone is sharp. "Now that they know, they won't let me out of their sight."

"I was scared shitless, Jenna. You have some crazy person after you, and when I couldn't get ahold of you, I panicked."

She walks into the kitchen, opens the fridge, grabs a bottle of white wine, and pours herself a generous glass. She leans against the counter and takes a long and slow sip. I stand opposite her, leaning against another counter.

"Robby." Jenna looks at me and pulls her lips into a line. "The judge called. They won't give me an order of protection."

My heart simultaneously shatters and grows with the need to protect her. Not even five minutes ago Jenna looked straight in Jake and Dax's eyes and said she hadn't heard from the judge yet. "What does this mean?"

She takes another sip of her wine, pours another glass, and holds it in front of her. "It means I have no protection from Eli right now. The judge didn't think his patterns proved he's a danger to me."

Jenna looks into her glass and runs a finger around the rim. "I need to ride it out. I should start hearing from journalism schools any day now. I hope I get into one or two, and then I'll move."

"Jenna." I take off my hat and run my hand through my hair. "That's a month. You're going to up and leave so soon?"

She looks down and shakes her head. "I was always going to leave at the end of the summer. You knew that."

It dawns on me for the first time that in a month Jenna and I will once again be headed in different directions. My interview with Teaching America went great today. I fully expect an offer and was told the four cities they are considering for me. They told me in no uncertain terms that I won't have a say in where they send me, and that it would be based on need. And only one of the cities lines up with Jenna's cities. I'll either be moving to Los Angeles, Miami, Charlotte, or New York City.

The chances that Jenna and I both end up in New York are slim. Our lives continue not to fit together, and I don't know why I thought or hoped that a night of great sex with change that. Especially after all she told me last night. She didn't mince words or lead me on. She made it clear that this is temporary.

Jenna studies me as my mouth falls open. Thoughts flood through me, but I finally pull myself together. "What can I do to help, Jenna?"

She smiles for the first time in a while. "I don't have much in my rental house, so I hope to donate most of the crap. But I'd love to crash here for as long as you're comfortable. Without an order of protection, I don't feel—"

"You know I'd love that." I don't let her continue.

Jenna puts her wine glass down, walks across the kitchen, and throws her arms around my neck. I wrap mine around her waist and hold her close. I kiss the top of her head and breathe her in.

She speaks into my neck. "I'm going to live my life and not let myself be intimated by this bullshit. And then I'm going to leave, and Eli will lose interest and harass someone else."

I tilt Jenna's chin up and kiss her with everything I have to offer. "You don't think Eli will back off?"

Jenna shakes her head. "They never do. I don't know if it's entitlement, a sickness, or what, but these men don't usually get it on their own."

Jenna sounds defeated, and I hate that this man is causing it. He's stealing her hope and joy, and the anger consumes me. Last night, everything changed between us. Yet, Jenna seems so hesitant to give us a real shot. She continues to talk about where she'll go next, and I fear last night changed nothing for her.

"We need to look at your computer." I grab the bag she threw when she got here. "We have to make sure Eli loses all access to you."

Jenna takes a deep breath. "And in less than a month, I'll find out where I'm going next."

We sit at her computer, running tests before we both give up, and Jenna decides she will buy herself a new laptop. She rests her feet on my lap, and I rub them, and she lays back with her computer. I can't quit thinking about the article I read, which, it turns out, Jenna wrote. It's hard to know that while I was back in Chicago, trying to get hold of her to apologize, she was here and dealing with all of that.

The Jenna I know wouldn't allow herself to be victimized. She is a badass, a strong woman, and the typical girl who was raised with two older brothers. She doesn't fit the profile for me. But what do I know about the characteristics of those abused by domestic partners? Maybe the women are always strong, like Jenna. And through time, they're broken down and made to believe they are less than they are.

The entire purpose of her op-ed piece was to show how strong victims are. No one asks if they can victimize someone, and strong people every day become victims at the hands of cowards and sick people. I pull my phone out of my pocket and put Eleanor Jenna's article in my search bar, and it comes up immediately. I reread it. This time, I glance at Jenna, the author who experienced all these things. And it clicks for me—all of it. We have to do better for our women. What we're doing isn't even close to good enough.

"Robby." Jenna's voice pulls me out of my thoughts, and she studies me. "What were you thinking about?"

"You," I say. It's not a lie. All I ever seem to think about these days is her. "You're the best friend I've ever had." And I won't let anything ruin that.

Chapter Twenty-Three

Jenna

*M*Y PHONE VIBRATES ON THE nightstand, and when I look, it's an unknown caller. I send it to voicemail. Twenty-seven missed calls from an unidentified number that started around two in the morning. Eli must have found my new number. Since breaking things off with him, I've already had to change it three times.

Robby still sleeps next to me. I turn my phone off, move to my side, and watch him. He lies on his side, and a strand of black hair falls in front of one of his eyes. Usually, he's so put together, but early in the mornings, Robby is undeniably himself. I love seeing him shirtless with his hair tousled. He's indisputably handsome and kissable.

When I ended things for good with Eli, I never thought I'd share a bed with a man again. And I don't mean celibacy. I mean the actual sharing of a bed. Even after my first time with Robby, I planned to go back to the guestroom to sleep. But then I stayed.

Sleeping was when I was most vulnerable. It's when things would happen. I'll never forget the first time I received a crash course in non-consensual sex within a relationship.

Yet as I lie here, watching Robby sleep, I've never felt safer. He would never hurt, violate, or convince me that I'm losing my mind because of how I feel. He's everything good—the golden standard.

Robby's eyes open to slits, and his lips turn up in a smile. "Are you watching me sleep, Jenna?"

My face flushes. Robby hooks me around my waist and pulls me close. My face burrows into his warm chest, and I breathe him in. Robby always smells like clean detergent. His strong arms hold me close until all the anxiety I had just felt over Eli having my phone number dissipates.

My therapist has repeatedly warned me about the PTSD I'd feel when I became intimate with a new person again. But I don't feel any PTSD as it relates to Robby. He's the first man I've been with since Eli, and there were no triggers. Only feelings of being safe and in control. Robby was the perfect person to do this with—probably, the only one it would have worked with. Everything Eli put me through changed how I look at people, including myself. She's been working to reprogram my thinking and remove all the triggers.

Robby kisses my forehead. "Shower. Café."

"Yeah." I kiss his chest. "Then I need to go to the paper. Jake is meeting me at the house with his truck, and I'll haul a few things to the donation center. Then my shift at The Pool Hall."

Robby moves his hand up the back of my shirt. "Sex. Shower. Café. Paper."

"Is this who we are now?" I roll Robby onto his back and straddle him. "Friends who have sex?"

Robby grips my arms, and looks at me so straight faced, that I can't tell what he's thinking. "This can be whatever you want it to be. You're calling the shots."

We've settled into playing house easily. Our patterns are similar to how we acted two summers ago. The only difference now is the sex. I sleep in Robby's room every night. It wasn't a conversation but an understanding. I go to the café with Robby, Sunny, and friends almost every morning. If I'm not working at The Pool Hall, we eat together, usually takeout, because neither of us cooks.

We don't talk about the future, but we both know our days are numbered. The chances of us ending up in the same place are slim. I've made enough bad decisions in the past few years. I'm not going to add following a guy and his career across the country. I'm finally prioritizing myself.

My phone rings and my body stiffens. When I look at the area code, I see it's a New York City number.

"This is Jenna," I say, picking up on the second ring.

"Jenna. Hi," a woman with a high-pitched voice says on the line. "It's Gabby. From *Harper's Bazaar*."

"Yes, hi. Hello." I clear my throat. I didn't know if I'd ever hear back on my latest submission and not this early. I jump out of the bed, throw a shirt on, and walk outside to take the call.

"We received your follow-up article, and wow, we were all blown away."

I pace back and forth on the grass. "Thank you. That means a lot."

"Jenna." Gabby pauses, and I can hear her breathing. "Going public with your real name, I want you, no, I need you to know, your life is about to change."

I've thought about this for a long time. It wasn't a split-second decision, but it's also not something I've discussed with people in my life, and it will affect them too.

"Gabby. I've been hiding from the truth for so long. If the courts won't give me my power and freedom back,

I need to take it."

"I agree." I can hear her smile through the phone. "But there is your life before the article and your life after."

"You're going to print it?"

"Jenna," Gabby says. "It's going to be our feature. And we'll include the stories that you sent along with your article. I can't believe how many women have reached out to the email address you created."

"Gabby," I put the phone up to my other ear. "I only sent about a third of them. There are so many."

She clears her throat. "I have to ask, what do you do with all of the emails? Isn't it heavy hearing all this stuff?"

"No," I sit down in a lawn chair. "It's not heavy. Because this stuff is happening, whether I get the emails or not, we all have a choice. We can move toward people's trauma to help them or look away."

"Do you write back?"

"To every single one of them." Robby pokes his head out of the cottage, and I lower my voice. "When will the feature run?"

"September issue. We want to come to Wheaton and do a photo session in the next few days, to accompany the article. If you're going to go public, we want your face as part of it. Only if you're okay with that."

"Thanks, Gabby." Blood drains from my face. This is what I want, but it's still scary.

"My team will be in touch by the end of the day with dates that will work to come to you."

My mind spins after the call ends, but I don't second-guess my decision to go public. After Jake moved back to Wheaton, it was a nightmare with all the news crews. I don't think my story will rise to that level, but I need to let my parents know. Jake and Camilla need to know, and Dax and Carrie. Not only that I'm going public, but I'm Eleanor Jenna. I haven't told any of them about the abuse; they only recently learned of the stalking. I need to prepare them for this, as there are details that won't be easy for them to hear.

And Robby. He needs to know too.

WORK TONIGHT IS A TYPICAL Thursday. Busy. Gavin is behind the bar, and I'm the only server on for the rest of the bar. Every time the bell rings on the door, I look up, hoping to see Robby, but my skin crawls when I see who it is instead. Eli walks in, and he and the guy he comes in with are both in their Rosso police uniforms.

Eli and I make eye contact, and then they sit at a round table in the corner.

"Gavin," I say as I head behind the bar. "That table in the corner is yours."

He glances up at me and nods his head. I appreciate that he doesn't ask questions.

The next person to walk in is Rafferty, the detective I talked to a few days ago. He's dressed casually now, not in his suit and tie, and he nods his head in my direction as he takes a seat at the bar.

"What can I get you?" I say, putting a napkin in front of him.

Rafferty points to our beers on tap. "Get me the darkest beer you have."

I put the beer in front of him, and without looking at me, he says, "I see your friend is here tonight."

"Yep." I take an order from the guy next to Rafferty and bring my attention back to him. "Which is completely within his legal rights. Meanwhile, he'll stare at me all night, make me feel uncomfortable, and I hope that he's not the last person standing because then I'll be here alone with him and his gun, and there isn't anything anyone can do to help me."

Rafferty pauses, holding his beer to his lips. "I've been going through camera footage of the brick in your car and the bar window."

"And." I lean closer.

"And every camera on Main Street works perfectly, but the night before your car was vandalized, the camera in front of The Pool Hall stopped working."

"Can I get a drink down here?" Someone from the other end of the bar yells. I hold a finger to Rafferty, fill some empty pint glasses, and then work my way back to him.

"Do you think someone did it on purpose?"

Rafferty leans forward. "The cord to the camera was cut. Yes. I think it was on purpose. And not only did we miss the brick to your car but also the one through the bar."

"Does that surprise you?" I put my hands on my hips. "Because when I filed a report with you, I got the impression you all protect your own."

Rafferty looks down, tapping his finger on the bar. "I hope Eli thinks that too."

He takes another sip of beer and stands up. "I've already been here too long. I believe you, Jenna. I'm doing my best to protect you, and we need to catch Eli in the act. I need proof."

He walks away without saying anything more.

The rest of the evening, I feel like a robot. I serve customers, avoiding contact with Eli, and think about my conversation with the detective. Catch him? How? It's all been unpredictable. And all the untraceable calls on my cell and at work.

The camera was conveniently vandalized before my car and the bar were. I already know it's Eli putting packages and letters in front of my door, but according to the judge, it doesn't matter that I feel threatened by that. It isn't unlawful. The judge made me feel like I was an alarmist for being scared. Isn't this always how a victim feels before the man shows up and kills her? Because that happens most the time.

Men like Judge Schuster are why many women don't bother to speak up. It's one thing to be victimized by a partner, but then to be revictimized by the people who are meant to protect us is next level. That's what Judge Shuster made me feel. Revictimized.

There was a time in my life when I didn't fully understand what being a victim of domestic abuse even meant. I didn't realize the terror that the victims went through. I remember thinking that something similar would never happen to me because I'd never enter into a relationship with someone who was capable of that level of abuse. I'm ashamed to admit it. But I'd hear stories and think, leave. That was easy for me to say. I'd never experienced anything remotely similar to abuse in my life. I always felt like I had the power.

Then I met Eli. We met right here, at The Pool Hall. And he was the first guy I felt a little excited about since my falling out with Robby. It felt good to feel a spark again. The abuse was so gradual that I didn't even realize it was happening. He isolated me from everyone in my life, and somehow, I became so reliant on him that it was hard to get out of it. Then the put-downs started. Those were gradual too, but I began to believe the lies he told me and eventually became convinced that no one else would love me.

The sex coercion then started. It's still hard for me to think of these things. When I ended things for good with Eli, I started seeing a therapist, and she used the word rape. Tears prick the back of my eyes as I invoke these memories. My therapist said that when I woke up from sleeping with Eli inside of me, and I didn't consent, that was rape. I tried to rationalize that too. We'd already slept together, so he was allowed to do this to me.

Rape is anything that isn't consensual. I know that. I've always known that. Yet when it was happening to me, I rationalized it. I told myself that it wasn't rape because we'd already been in a relationship together that involved consensual sex. Rape can and does happen in the comfort of your home and bed, such as waking up to a man on top and inside of you, refusing to get off because he is so close. Rape can take on so many forms. Like, drinking too much, and passing out, only to wake up with your pants around your ankles and a man inside of you. Rape happens more frequently, and in different forms. I learned that from my parents and in school, yet when it was happening to me, I talked myself into thinking it was okay.

Eli never hit me, but I think it would have escalated to that point too. He started to be more handsy. A push here, squeezing my arm hard enough that I bruised. I stayed through all of it. I convinced myself that nothing I was going through was a big deal. And now he's stalking me, and I have no rights.

"Jenna." I'm brought back to reality by the sound of my name. I look around the bar, and it's nearly empty. Gavin is cleaning the tables.

It's Eli standing in front of me. I choke on my breath. "I don't want to talk to you."

He steps closer, and I glance at Gavin behind me as he reaches into his pocket, puts his phone on the table, and then steps away.

Eli smirks. "I have it on good authority that you tried to get an order of protection against me."

It's true. I have no privacy. He's a cop. He knows everything. I'm helpless.

I blow out a breath. "Well, if that's what you heard, it must be true."

Eli laughs. He's smug. "I'd be real careful, Jenna, about your next move."

"Meaning?" I put my hands on my hips and feign confidence.

"Meaning I have a lot of friends in very high places."

I take a step closer to the table where Gavin left his phone. "I'm out of options. You leave letters at my house. You follow me around town. You call and hang up on me." I leave out the fact that he's also throwing bricks at things.

"What do you expect from me, Jenna." Eli steps closer. "I love you. I miss you. We could work all of this out if you'd sit down and talk to me."

Rafferty's words echo in my ear. I need proof, but how. "Eli, I'm only going to say this one more time. When we were together, you were abusive. I finally found the courage to get the hell out. And now I want nothing more than for you to leave me alone. There is no us. There will never be an us. And your presence scares me."

Then I spew out. "Get help."

Eli frowns, but then his lips turn up into a maniacal smile. He puts his hand on his gun, and I hold my breath. He's always flashed his gun around me as if I needed the reminder that it's there and that he's not scared to use it. "What, Jenna? You want me to step aside while you go around town and whore it up with that preppy-ass city boy?"

"Leave him—"

"Are you fucking him?" Eli cuts me off. "What's his name, Robby Bergland, is it?"

I charge Eli. I push him. Actually, I try to push him, but he doesn't budge because he's a massive wall. He grabs me by my wrists.

"You be careful, Jenna. And tell Robby to watch his back too."

Eli lets go of me and turns to walk out the door.

"Wait," I call after him. "What does that mean? Why should I be careful?"

"Because if I can't have you, no one will."

The door slams, and I collapse to the floor. Tears flood my eyes, and I try to blink them away.

Gavin rushes to me, pulls me to my feet, and wraps his arms around me. I cry into his shoulder.

Gavin glances at his phone. "I think I got it. All of it." He motions toward his phone.

The door opens again, and my eyes meet Robby's. He looks at Gavin and then at me. Gavin spins me toward him, Robby wraps his arm around me, and I finally feel safe.

Chapter Twenty-Four

Robby

THIS PAST WINTER, I WAS in my Primrose Hill flat in London, mindlessly scrolling through my social media feeds, while it pissed sleet outside my window. An article kept popping up, so I finally tapped on it. I read the article that Jenna wrote under the pen name Eleanor Jenna.

I don't remember all the details of the article, but I do remember it being beautifully written. Poignant. A picture accompanied the article and was the silhouette of a woman, backlit, so none of her features were identifiable.

I never thought about the piece again. Not until Jenna told me she was the author. I feel like I've been let into an intimate part of her life I was never supposed to know about. I can't blame myself, but if I hadn't been an ass two summers ago, maybe Jenna and I would have been together, and there would never have been an Eli.

It's been three nights since Eli approached her at The Pool Hall, and it's been two days since she handed over the recording to the judge, seeking again to get an order of protection. We've all rallied around her and aren't letting her out of our sight. Right now, she's at her parents' house. Jake, Camilla, Dax, and Carrie are there too. She said she wanted to talk to me next.

While I wait for Jenna to text or call, I head over to my grandparents' home. Sis is sitting at the table in the kitchen when I arrive. Her hair still has curlers in it, and I kiss her cheek.

"How are you today, Grandma?"

"Robby." She holds her teacup to her lips. "I'm afraid I'm rather confused."

She puts her hand over mine. "I talked to your dad this morning. They said they're coming, but I can't remember for what holiday."

"Labor Day, Grandma." I look up as Sunny shuffles into the room. "Dad and Mom will come for the weekend, so will your son Larry and his wife Diane. We're going to help you move to Pelican Crest."

"Remember Sis," Sunny says, putting a hand on the center island for support. "We're moving there. We looked at the room. It was nice, and they had people there that would help us. This place is too big, and we've gotten too old."

Sis's shoulders drop as she looks around. "But Sunny, we raised Rob and Larry here. We're going to throw that all away?"

Grandma Sis brings up my dad, Rob, who I'm named after.

"Sis." Sunny sits at the table with us. "We aren't throwing anything away. We're downsizing."

Her eyes well up with tears, and she studies her hands in her lap. "But where will everyone stay when they visit Wheaton?"

"That's what the cottage is for, dear." Sunny removes Sis's glasses and wipes her eyes with a tissue. "We don't need this big old house. Let a younger family enjoy it."

When I arrive at the cottage in the late afternoon,

Jenna is sprawled out on a lawn chair, reading a book. Seeing Jenna is like arriving home.

She smiles. "It's too beautiful out to be indoors."

I look up at the sky, and there isn't a cloud. I don't care what we do as long as I'm with Jenna.

"What'd you have in mind?" I ask as she stands up, and I wrap my arms around her and kiss her.

"I'm up for anything," she says.

"Any interest in boating to the resort? We could grab dinner at the docks and bring a bottle of wine. Get some sun," I suggest.

"That sounds perfect," Jenna says.

I turn to go into the cottage. "I'll put my trunks on. Want to start packing a basket?"

We head out onto the lake in my grandpa's small but cozy boat. The motor isn't very big, so even at full throttle, it will take a while to get there. Jenna sits next to me as I drive.

"How was the family meeting?" I address the elephant in the room.

Jenna takes a long sip of wine from her yeti cup. "Good. Everyone was supportive." She pauses, and her eyes find mine. "I wanted to talk to them first. Before talking to you."

I don't say anything, but I get it. They're her family. I'm not sure what I am to Jenna, but I know what she's become to me.

"Well." She bites her bottom lip, always the sign that she's nervous about something. "I submitted a follow-up article to *Harper's Bazaar*. They will print it in their September issue as a feature."

"Jenna." I turn the motor off and stand to hug her. "I am so proud of you."

"There's one more thing, Robby." She backs away but keeps her hands on my shoulders. "I'm going to go public with my identity."

Thoughts flood my mind. What this is going to mean for her. How this could change the trajectory of her life. Actually, not could. This will change everything. Pride floods every ounce of me.

"Let me know what you need from me." I kiss her. "How can I best support you?"

Jenna looks at me, and her eyes smile.

"You amaze me, Jenna Abram. Everything about you. I ..."

I stop talking because I feel dangerously close to emotions flooding out of me, so instead, I pull her close and nuzzle my face in her hair. Jenna inspires me and makes me want to be a better person. She's been through so much but is strong. She could shut down; instead, she's become the voice for people who don't have their own.

She's a survivor in every sense of the word, and somehow, she thinks I'm worthy of being in her presence. She forgave me and I've never been happier than I have these past couple of weeks of getting to be with Jenna. All of her.

Jenna pulls away and wipes her eye. "I'm sorry. I don't know why I'm emotional. I knew you'd support me. Thank you, Robby. I felt I needed your acceptance to move forward with this for some reason."

"You don't need my acceptance."

"I needed your support, though. Having you in my camp makes me feel strong."

"Same, Jenna." I sit back down and start the motor.

We get to the resort, and a waitress comes to the dock. We don't even have to get out of the boat. Jenna and I order a walleye sandwich, and instead of eating at the resort, we decide to take it in the boat to go.

We return to the cottage, and Jenna turns on the outside radio to an oldies station. I go inside, grab a bottle of wine, and pour us both a glass. I take a sip, then put it down, and hold Jenna's hand as we dance badly to a Bob Dylan song, laughing as I spin her.

"I can't wait to hear back from the schools. Any day now." Jenna gives me a wine-soaked kiss.

"If there were one school, one city you'd like above all else, what would you choose?" I like to play this game with Jenna. I enjoy pretending we control our fate.

Jenna furrows her eyebrows. "I've been thinking a lot about this. Columbia."

"New York City." I nod. I can see Jenna there.

She continues. "They have one of the best documentary journalism master's programs."

The song changes, and it's something upbeat by The Beach Boys. "I want to bring voices to people."

"You don't seem like a Morningside Heights girl, but maybe you could live on the upper west side, take the subway to school every day, and spend your evenings gallivanting around the city."

"Robby." Jenna stops dancing, picks up her glass, and takes a drink. "It sounds dreamy."

I often think about what life would look like if Jenna and I landed in New York. I have decided to rent my condo in Chicago, which will also provide additional income.

New York City is so gentrified, and the neighborhoods I'll be needed in won't be the upper west side. It may not be in Manhattan at all. I'd gladly live anywhere to be near Jenna. I'm not sure she's in the same place as me. Sometimes when she talks, it's as if she wants to leave everything behind, and I worry that everything includes me.

Chapter Twenty-Five

Jenna

ROBBY AND I WENT TO bed at four in the morning. There was so much to talk about, many songs to dance to, and so much wine to drink. When his alarm goes off at eight, he leans over and kisses my temple.

"You sleep in. I'll go to the café with the boys alone today."

I say something inaudible, Robby walks out, and I hear the shower turn on. I doze off and barely register him shuffling around the room. He's probably ironing a Gucci t-shirt, cause well, that's Robby.

The bed dips, but I don't move or open my eyes. I need about a hundred more hours of sleep. He kisses my head, his hand warm on my shoulder.

"Have a great day." It's a faint whisper.

There is no falling back asleep after that. When I hear the door close, I sit up.

My phone rings from an unidentified Wheaton number. "This is Jenna."

"Hi, Jenna." A female's voice echoes out on the other

end. "This is Judge Kepler."

"Uh, hi." The last judge I spoke to was male. I don't know a Judge Kepler.

"First," she says. "I want to let you know that your order of protection was granted."

"Wait. What?" I sit up straighter. "He's been served? Is it over?"

"He hasn't been served yet," the judge says. "But the order has been handed over to law enforcement, so that should be in the works as we speak."

"How long is the restraining order good for?"

"Two years."

There's silence on both ends and then an audible breath. "And Jenna?"

"Yes."

"I want to apologize that you weren't set up with a victim's advocate like you should have been. I'm not sure how this fell through the cracks, but I'm sorry."

Relief hits me in all the places where fear once lived. I somehow mutter a thank you and then I cry. No, I sob. I've been on edge for so long that I disassociated from everything. Well, until Robby came back and charmed the pants off me.

That's what people don't understand. How many people in my position change their lives? No one fully understands what living in constant fear does to a person. I've stepped away from relationships, lost myself, and looked around every corner in fear.

I pull myself together and start packing my bags. Staying at the cottage with Robby was always temporary. It made me feel safe being out here, but now that my order of protection has been granted, there's no need.

Robby walks through the door, his hands full of bags from the grocery store. When our eyes meet, his smile extends across his face, and I almost wonder if he'll miss having me here. We get along so well, and the company has been great.

Then his face changes when he sees my bag on a chair.

"A judge called." I rub a hand over my face. "The order of protection against Eli is being served as we speak."

Robby drops his bags on the table and walks to me, arms extended. "Great, Jenna. This is what needed to happen."

He pulls me into a hug, and I breathe into his shirt. "I was here to feel safe, and now that the restraining order has been granted, I should really finish out the summer in my house."

Robby runs a finger down my cheek. "It's up to you, Jenna. You don't have to. I love having you here."

"And I appreciate that." I squeeze his hand before walking to where my bag is, packed and ready to go. "I've been here almost two weeks and have about a million things to do. I need to prepare to live somewhere else. I need to finish out my shifts and the bar, and the paper, and—"

"I'm a distraction." Robby leans against the peninsula in the kitchen.

"A good distraction." I walk to him and kiss his cheek. "But this was always going to be temporary."

Robby looks at his bags on the table. I glance too, and food spills out of them. I don't know what he wants out of this, but I know that I should hear any day now what school I got into, and spending this much time with Robby is confusing. I feel on the brink of putting my dreams aside to follow him wherever he goes. I've done this before, and Robby isn't promising me a future. It's not a topic we've ever discussed, but the more time I spend with him, the more I think I want it, which is why I need to leave.

"We'll still see each other. We'll both be here for another month."

Robby smiles and takes my hand. "You're right."

Chapter Twenty-Six

Robby

THE COTTAGE IS EERILY QUIET without Jenna here. After she leaves, I put all the groceries away. I thought it would be fun to cook, but Jenna had other plans. I text Camilla to see if she, Jake, and Signe are free for dinner, as I don't want the food to go to waste.

Camilla walks through the door with Signe a few hours later, and it looks like a bomb went off in the kitchen. I'm not even sure if this meal will be edible. In Chicago, delivery services can bring the best food the city has to offer at the press of a button, so I've never spent much time learning how to cook. I thought it would be fun to do this with Jenna, but it's a disaster.

"Can I help with anything?" Camilla looks around. There are half-cut vegetables everywhere, sauce on the walls from being overly boiled, and I haven't even made the noodles yet.

"I'm wondering if I should abort the mission and order us pizzas?"

Camilla laughs and hands me Signe. She smiles, and I nuzzle my face into Signe's neck, and she laughs.

"Where's Jake?" I ask.

"He's still on a job." Camilla puts water in a pan and turns the burner on. "Where's Jenna?"

"She's back at her place in town." I sigh. "The order of protection was granted this morning."

"That's great." Camilla wipes the sauce off the walls and then starts cutting what's left of the vegetables. "It is great, isn't it, Robby?"

"Well, yeah, of course." I don't hesitate. This is what we all wanted for Jenna.

"Then why do you look like your cat just died?"

Signe starts to fuss, so I pace with her. She always likes to be in motion. "It was nice having her here. This summer is flying by, and it's almost over."

Camilla dumps noodles into the boiling water and stirs. "Do you want it all to be over?"

"The summer ends when the summer ends, Cam. Even I can't change that."

She throws a towel at me. "Do you want things to end with Jenna?"

I face Signe outward so she can look at her mama while I hold her. "What do you mean?"

"Don't play dumb with me," Camilla says. "I know something is going on between the two of you."

"What?" I feign surprise and wrinkle my nose. "I don't know what you're talking about."

Camilla raises and eyebrow and crosses her arms over her chest. "There is zero part of me that believes you or that will entertain this conversation. I'm your sister. Spill."

Everyone probably knows. We spend every moment together. She's been staying at the cottage for nearly two weeks. She goes to coffee with the men and me almost every day. It's not a relationship I've talked about with anyone, even Camilla. Everything is still so unclear in my head that it doesn't feel right to say things out loud until I've fully processed what this relationship is to me.

"Honestly," I finally answer. "I don't know what we are to each other."

Camilla strains the noodles, fills us both a bowl and pours sauce over the noodles. Then brings the salad she somehow salvaged to the table. She takes Signe from me.

"When I was falling for Jake," she says. "I convinced myself that how I felt wasn't important because my life was somewhere else."

I shoot up when I smell something burning. I'd forgotten about the garlic bread. I open the oven and pull out the very burned, not salvageable bread. Smoke fills the room, and I open a few windows to let the fresh air in.

"The difference is, Jake wanted you to stay. And you knew that." I pull open the door as well because the cottage has gotten so smoky.

Camilla studies me. "And Jenna doesn't want you to?"

"Jenna," I remind her. "Doesn't know where she's going to end up. You're correct. No part of her has asked me to come along."

"Ask her."

"Well, that reeks of desperation."

Camilla shakes her head. "Yeah, because being lovesick while not knowing where you stand with someone seems much better, Robby."

"I'm not lovesick." I motion toward the table, and we take a seat. I look at the pathetic meal I tried to put together.

"Keep telling yourself that." Camilla balances Signe on her lap, and spoons noodles into her mouth with her free hand.

Later that evening, long after Camilla and Signe have left and after the cottage is cleaned from my disaster, Jenna shows up. She knocks once and then walks through the door. Our eyes meet.

"Robby, the emails came through." She holds her new laptop in her hand. I smile and motion for her to sit on the couch and join her.

"I got notified that there were system changes to all five of my applications." Jenna puts her hand over her mouth. "I think a decision's been made."

She squeezes her laptop against her chest, and I point to it. "Okay, here we go."

"But." Her smile falters. "I'm freaking out. I want to open the emails, but I'm scared to."

"Let's do it together." I pull her across the couch, closer to me. "The sooner you know, the sooner you can start planning what's next."

She balances her laptop and clicks on the first online application. "Vanderbilt University."

Jenna scrolls, and then her eyes light up. "We are happy to inform you that you've been accepted into our winter session beginning in January."

"Robby." She throws her hands up and tackles me into a hug. "I got into Vanderbilt. I could be moving to Nashville."

"Okay, the next school is the University of Texas in Austin." She smiles immediately. "In."

Jenna yells it like it's the most surprising thing in the world. How can Jenna be so goddamn perfect and oblivious to it?

"Okay, University of Georgia, here I come." She once again launches herself into my lap. Three schools. Three acceptances.

"Now you only need to hear from Columbia and De

Paul," I say, getting up and grabbing a bottle of wine to celebrate.

She stands up too. "I didn't think I'd have options. I was hoping for one school, but now I need to do research. Do I want warm weather? Or more of a city vibe?"

At the end of the month, we'll both be somewhere else. And when her latest article gets published in *Harper's Bazaar*, I have no doubt her life will change. She'll be in high demand and a celebrity wherever she decides to live.

I pour us both a glass of wine. "I can help you research cities if you'd like."

She nods. "Or I'll wait a day or two to hear from Columbia. Because if I get in there, I will not entertain the other ones."

Jenna takes my hand and leads me outside, and we sit in the late summer sun and look at the lake. There is so much I want to say, but I don't want to make anything about me when we should celebrate Jenna. Instead, I think about everything I want to experience with her in our last few weeks of summer in Wheaton before our lives take us in very different directions.

Chapter Twenty-Seven

Jenna

I HEAR FROM COLUMBIA UNIVERSITY IN New York City two days later, and I know what the next stage of my life will look like. There is so much peace in knowing where I'm going to live.

I even signed a lease on an apartment that I found online. The pictures look gorgeous and it's available September first. It's a little out of my preferred neighborhood and is instead in South Harlem, but it's close to Columbia, and a short walk from Central Park. And even though the price is right, this one-bedroom is still the most expensive place I'll have lived. My favorite part about the building is that it has a doorman. I may be in a good place, but I will sleep better at night having that extra protection.

Even though I didn't get accepted until the semester beginning in January, I want to get to know the city for a few months, which is why I'll leave at the end of the summer.

The next day, I'm at Jake and Camilla's house, waiting for the photographers from *Harper's Bazaar* to show up. I wanted to make sure it was somewhere not in town to ensure people weren't talking. The view of the lake is gorgeous—a perfect backdrop for a photo shoot.

A stunning woman walks out of the SUV, and we meet each other halfway on the lawn.

"You must be Jenna. I'm Gabby." She shakes my hand, and her smile is warm.

I take in her perfect and crisp button-up shirt, tucked into her long, white pants, and shiny red flats. "Welcome to Wheaton. I hope you found it okay."

Two more women get out of the SUV, both with large cameras, and they start doing some lighting tests. "You were right that this is nowhere near an airport."

I chuckle. "Not even close."

Another woman gets out of the SUV, holding a large briefcase.

"I'm Aubrey. I'll be doing your hair and makeup."

"Hair and makeup," I repeat, raising an eyebrow. "I didn't realize I'd be getting the star treatment."

"This is so exciting, Jenna." Camilla hugs my arm.

I walk Gabby inside and show Aubrey where she can set up. Camilla asked if she could be here because she's obsessed with this entire process, and Jake is at work.

We sit around the kitchen island, and Aubrey works on my hair. Gabby sits next to me.

"Are you ready for this, Jenna?"

It's a hard question for me to answer and one I've been asked many times over the past few days. The problem with going public is that I don't want this article to be about me. I want it to be about everyone. But in not going public, domestic abuse remains an abstract idea for most people. My family had all read the article under my pseudonym, and it remained abstract. Although not in my comfort zone, being the face of this could lead to not only my freedom, but other women's as well.

"I honestly don't know," I say.

Aubrey runs a wand through my hair.

"In some ways, it feels like you're taking on the police force." She puts gloss in my hair that makes it shine.

I shake my head. "People will draw conclusions, but I don't want that to be the angle. Yes, my abuser happens to be a cop, but it was the police force of Wheaton that helped serve the order of protection. That's important too."

Gabby smiles. "We try hard not to have an angle. We're printing your story as is. And then, we dedicated several pages to the email chain you sent. You're going to change the narrative, Jenna. I hope you realize that."

"I'd settle for other victims' stories being a greater narrative. That's what success looks like to me."

After my hair and makeup, they agree to let me wear a purple dress I bought for this occasion to stand in solidarity with everyone else who has been impacted by domestic abuse. We walk to the lake, where they take many pictures of me.

Gabby gives me a long hug as we part. She holds me for a beat longer than I expect, and there is warmth and maybe even understanding in her embrace. She then pulls away. "Did I hear you're Columbia bound?"

"Yes." I smile. "Moving the first of September."

She hands me her card. "New York is going to love you, and you are going to love New York. I'd love to grab a coffee when you get to town. Introduce you around. I'm also a transplant, and it can be hard to get to know people."

I cover my smiling mouth with my hand. "I'm going to take you up on that."

I did not expect to know someone in New York on day one. As I wave to Gabby and the crew, I can barely contain my joy.

CAMILLA AND JAKE HAVE EVERYONE over for a cookout to celebrate their joint birthdays. They were born the same day, ten years apart. It's quite the story. They kept it to family this year, and I sit on the blanket, helping support Signe, who is still not sitting on her own. Carrie and Kylie come to sit by me.

"Why do you have to move to New York?" Kylie sticks her bottom lip out. "That's at least ten states away."

I stick my finger out, and poke Kylie in the nose. "You can visit me there anytime. And I'll come back a lot, I promise."

"But Auntie Jenna." Kylie throws her hands up in the air.

"My school is there," I tell her. "And it's a really good school, and it will be an adventure."

Signe squawks, and I lie her down on her back and play with her feet. I've been so focused on being excited for my next journey that I hadn't thought about how hard it would be to be on the other side of the country away from these people. Everyone is here. And then there's Robby. And I feel like the two of us are floating out there somewhere, stuck between here and there.

Robby comes and sits by me on the blanket and picks Signe up. "Is Auntie Jenna telling you lies about me again?"

"They've never been lies." I glance at him, and he's staring back and me, and he smiles.

"I dressed down for you today." Robby points to his crisp blue T-shirt.

"It's got a Gucci emblem on it." I pull at the label right above the front pocket. "It doesn't count."

Robby laughs as puts Signe on his knees and rocks onto his back, bouncing her in the air "Auntie Jenna doesn't appreciate good fashion, Signe."

When Signe starts to fuss, Carrie takes her. "Poor baby," she says. "Always stuck in the middle of this Jenna-Robby banter."

I lie back in the grass, too, and meet his gaze. Robby blocks his eyes from the sun. "You have two weeks left in this place."

"You make it sound like I'll never come back." I pick at the grass.

Robby's lips move to a thin line. "You won't come back. You'll visit, but Jenna, you won't ever be back. At least, not how you're here now."

"Time to sing," Kylie yells out from the picnic table across the lawn, and jolts Robby and I out of this conversation. He puts his arms out to me, helps me up, and we join the others singing for Jake and Camilla.

"How you doing, kiddo?" My dad wraps his arm around me as I reach the table. We all start to sing happy birthday.

"Good," I respond after. "The house is empty, and I'm not taking anything with me except the clothes on my back."

For some reason, I'm most scared for my dad to learn about the things that went on in my relationship with Eli. There is something about fathers and daughters, and I know he's going to put the burden on himself, but it doesn't belong there. Sometimes bad things happen, and nothing can be done about it.

After the celebration, Robby and I walk back to the cottage. Neither of us says anything, but the silence is comfortable. Neither of us seems to have the need to fill the space with words that don't matter or carry importance. He reaches over, takes my hand, and laces his fingers through mine.

"How did John take it when you gave notice at the paper?" Robby looks at me.

"He was very understanding. Thinks I'm going to put *Wheaton Happenings* on the map. Says it will be good for paper circulation."

"I think he's right." We reach the cottage, and Robby holds the door open for me. "I can't believe you already leave in two weeks."

I put my hands through the back pockets of his shorts and kiss him. "I know."

"But we haven't had sex the three million times I was hoping for." Robby grins and tucks a strand of hair behind my ear. "Jenna?"

I put my hand on his face, which turns serious as he stares back at me. "Yeah?"

His mouth falls open, like he's about to say something, but then he shakes the thought away. He leans forward and kisses me. Slowly. His lips press against mine, and electricity passes between us like every other time. It's this undeniable sensation where it's always unspoken that this won't end in only a kiss. It will always be more than that—just like our relationship was never only going to be a friendship.

Our kiss deepens, Robby's hand goes to the back of my neck, and he glides his fingers through my hair. Our breathing becomes erratic, and I reach down, pull his shirt over his head, and kiss his chest. And collarbone and shoulders. I want to memorize and remember everything about his body.

Without pulling away from our kiss, Robby leads me to the bedroom.

"I guess it won't hurt if I stay at the cottage one more time." We finish taking off each other's clothes.

Instead of getting into bed, Robby starts sprinkling my face with light kisses. First on my forehead, and then my eyes, the tip of my nose, my cheeks, the delicate place where my jaw meets my ear. Robby then moves down to my collarbone, my chest, and then my stomach. Neither of us acknowledge it, but each kiss feels like a goodbye.

Robby lifts me, and I wrap my legs around his waist. He lies me back in bed and props himself up on an elbow and stares at me so intently, that my face and body start to heat from the attention.

"Who says friends can't have sex without complicating things." When the words escape my lips, Robby's eyes seem to fill with tears.

"Right." He nods.

I reach up to pull his head toward me, and kiss him so hard, that the only air he breathes is sourced by me. Robby's hard body presses against mine, and I open my legs for him, and tug at his hair as he fills me in all the places I hadn't realized were empty.

He moves over me in a slow and methodical motion, like waves gently crashing onto a sandy beach, all the same size, all displacing the same amount of water. Robby pulls away from our kiss, and cups my face, and we stare at each other.

I notice every angle on his face, and how his dark hair falls over his face with each thrust of his hips. I glance at his full lips, extra pink and plump from all the kisses. I move my hand to his muscular back and trace my index finger down the straight line of his spine.

And then I look back into his eyes, which haven't left mine. They are so dark and hold so much. They are the road to everything that makes Robby who he is. They look a little sad to me.

"Hey." I push his hair out of his face so I can get a better look at him. "Are you okay?"

The words come out ragged, because it's hard to have a logical thought when Robby continues to rub against my core the way he's doing. A slow and steady stream of pleasure.

"You are so beautiful." After the words come out of his mouth, he presses his forehead into mine, and pushes into me harder.

My orgasm comes on so gradually, that I don't feel it coming, but then it hits me all at once. The waves are no longer steady but a tidal wave, and when I arch my back, my hips crash against Robby's, and neither of us wants to let go first. The pleasure ripples through me, until I have no choice but to collapse back on the bed, and Robby falls onto me a second later.

Our hearts race against each other's, and somehow, I think, this time felt different from all the others. With very little words, we told each other how much we value this unnamed thing between us. And now, more than I've ever been, I feel ready to move forward.

Chapter Twenty-Eight

Robby

THERE'S STILL NO WORD FROM Teaching America, which means in two weeks, after the Labor Day holiday, I'll head back to Chicago and wait until I hear something. I may even have to take a job at Goldman Sachs during the waiting period. After all the anticipation this summer, wondering where I'd end up and if it would be in the same place as Jenna, it looks like we're headed in different directions.

This isn't how I wanted things to end between us, but we haven't figured out the relationship thing while we're both in the same town. The possibility that she'd be up for a long-distance relationship as she's learning a new city is probably slim.

Sunny and I walk to the café, and he turns to me. "Why hasn't Jenna joined us the last few days?"

My interactions with Jenna have become less. I know it's because she's busy preparing, but I also think it's part of our long goodbye.

"She's moving soon, Grandpa. She has a lot to prepare for." We reach the café, and I open the door for him. "And she has Dax and Carrie's wedding to help plan, and then she has to pack up for her big move. She's busy."

"You kids," Sunny says as we walk to the usual table to meet the guys. "You're always too busy to look up and see things directly in front of you."

I'm quiet, but I observe the men and their conversations. Sunny's words stick with me. If it were only up to me, I would ask Jenna to be my girlfriend, and I'd do long distance while I worked on my plan to get to New York. If I land a job at Teaching America, and it's in another city, maybe I could see about transferring to Goldman Sachs in New York or finding another investment banking job there.

I hate investment banking, and now I'd be living in a city to be near Jenna, but no closer to my dreams than I was before. But I'd be with Jenna, and that'd be enough. I'm at a point in my life where I'd gladly take the back burner to someone else's career aspirations. I've lost Jenna once, and I don't want to do it again.

"Hey, guys." I stand up. "I remembered I have something I need to do. I'll see you all tomorrow."

"Is everything okay?" Sunny says, glancing up at me as he pats the side of his mouth with a napkin.

I look toward the door. "Yep. But there's something I need to do. I'll catch up with you later."

Sunny smiles, and I leave and drive to Jenna's.

Her car is parked out front, and I take a deep breath and knock on her door. I'm unsure what to say, but I must say something. I knock, but she doesn't immediately answer. I knock once more and think I hear footsteps. I move my face closer to the door.

"Jenna, it's me," I call through the closed door before knocking a final time. "I hear you in there. Are you okay?"

It sounds like something drops, and the hair stands up on my arms. I turn the knob of Jenna's front door, but it's locked. "Jenna. Let me in." I can feel the presence of her on the other side of the door.

Jenna peeks her head out, but the only opens the door a crack, and stands there. "Hey, Robby. What's up?"

Her voice is clipped. "Is everything okay?" I ask her. "I thought I heard a struggle."

"Yeah." She continues to stare at me. "I'm really busy today, though."

I stuff my hands in my pocket. "Can we talk?"

She's so beautiful, even in her casual leggings, tank top, and her bare feet. Her blond hair is pulled on top of her head, and she takes my breath away. I want to tell her everything I've been feeling. I want to offer to follow her wherever she goes, but I need to say it in a way that doesn't scare her. After everything Jenna has been through, I've been nervous to come on too strong, but everything I feel for her is becoming too difficult to contain.

Jenna pulls her lips into a straight line and takes a long blink. "I'd like to say something to you first."

"Okay." I nod.

Jenna looks at me, her face unreadable, and her hand on the frame of the door. "This thing between us needs to end. Whatever it was."

My body feels like it's been tased. Everything is fuzzy. Her words stab me.

Jenna continues. "My life is headed in a very different direction than yours. I think it's confusing if we continue to hang out like we have been. I'm leaving, and we need a clean break."

"Jenna," I say her name slowly, waiting for my brain and voice to be on the same page. "You don't want to see me anymore? In any capacity?"

She shakes her head. "You're a distraction, and not to mention in the way. I've had a specific plan, and you don't fit into it."

Jenna's voice is void of any emotion. She looks at me, and I don't know how I could have been so wrong about things with her. I don't know exactly what I planned to tell her when I arrived, but I think it was along the lines of I'd do anything for her and go anywhere too. I think that's what I wanted to say.

"You can move on and pretend that nothing happened between us?" I drag my hand down my face.

"Nothing happened." Jenna holds tightly to the door. "I'm sorry if you felt differently."

"Nothing happened?" I repeat her words.

The summer flashes before my eyes. No one is that good of an actor. Something happened. No one can fake the kind of connection that Jenna and I felt. The connection that I came here to tell her I feel. How could I have been so wrong about this?

"Robby," she says. "I am really busy, so if there's nothing else you need." Jenna looks beyond me, toward my car. She seems eager for me to leave.

"Umm, no." I start backing away from the door, too stunned to say anything else. "Are you sure you're okay?"

Jenna hesitates, only for a moment, and then nods. "Bye, Rob."

I turn on my heels and walk to my car. I look back at her house, and the door is already closed. I get in and drive down the street, replaying our entire conversation. I didn't come here expecting Jenna to drop everything to be with me, but I wanted to let her know how I felt. I didn't realize I was the only one struggling with my feelings. She's done. Maybe, she never even started.

Nothing happened. I'm a distraction. She called me Rob. Why would she call me Rob? No one calls me that—literally, no one. I've only ever been Robby. Jenna was stiff. She looked a little pale. She didn't seem like herself at all. I slam on my breaks, and with trembling figures, I pull Detective Rafferty's card out of my wallet and call him. He answers on the first ring.

"Detective Rafferty, this is Robby Bergland." My voice shakes as I talk.

I tell him the details of what happened. I can't be positive, but I don't think Jenna is okay. I let him know that something seemed very off with the entire interaction. If Jenna doesn't want to see me anymore, I accept that, but I'll never forgive myself if she is in danger and I don't do anything."

"Don't go back there," Rafferty says. "I'm sending the police immediately."

I keep my promise and don't go back, but I do park down the street. My hair is now sticking up all over my body again, and I can't shake the feeling I have that Jenna isn't okay. I watch as unmarked police vehicles pull up on the other end of the road and officers get out and surround the house. Detective Rafferty shows up, too, in a suit and tie. One of the officers approaches the door, and I hold my breath and wait.

Will Jenna answer and tell everyone that she's fine and that just because she doesn't want to continue things with me, it doesn't mean her life is in danger? I'd much prefer that option to the one where her life is in danger. I'd rather have sounded the alarm on all of these officers than have Jenna in harm's way.

She doesn't come to the door. The knocking turns into pounding. "Eli, if you're in there, come out with your hands up."

Nothing. I call Dax first. Then I call Jake, who is going to call their parents. Everyone is now on their way to Jenna's rental house.

Chapter Twenty-Nine

Jenna

I'M CALMER THAN I SHOULD be, but I think that's because I always knew Eli would find me. No order of protection was going to keep him away. At the same time, though, when there was a knock at my door this morning, my guard was down. I didn't even ask who it was. I knew who I'd hoped it would be. I flung it open, and Eli stood there. I've been on guard constantly, and for a mere moment, I allowed myself to be normal, and to think hope was on the other side of things.

Eli almost had me through the back door, where his car waited when the police showed up and surrounded the place. If they had arrived even thirty seconds later, I'd be in a car somewhere with Eli, and I think that would have been it for me. Because where does a person go from here? How does a person come back from this?

Robby must have called the police. When he came to the door, Eli had only been there about five minutes. And he told me if I didn't find a way to get rid of Robby, he'd kill him. I couldn't let that happen, so I stood there and lied better than I thought capable. I watched as his face crumpled, and I felt like I could see his heart breaking.

And in my last attempt at conveying something to him, I called him Rob. I've never called him Rob.

Eli peeks out from my bedroom, where my hands and feet are now tied together. Maybe I only feel calm because I've resolved myself to my fate. This will end like so many other domestic abuse scenarios. Eli will kill me, then turn the gun on himself. I'll become another statistic. I'll be another woman on a poster, and people will glance at it but then move on with their day because we've all become so desensitized to the violence. There is a huge part of me that knew this would happen.

"Stay still." Eli looks at me and then peeks into the hallway. I hear footsteps outside my bedroom window. I don't know how many officers are here, but we're surrounded.

"There's no way out." My words are quiet, matter of fact, and Eli's eyes dart to mine.

"Fuck, fuck, fuck." He holds his gun and looks at it. "Fuck." He says it louder this time.

"Can I ask you a question?"

Eli looks at me, and it's as if a stranger is looking back at me. I've disassociated from the fact that I once dated him.

"Why me?" My back presses against the headboard. "You're a good-looking guy. Relationships don't always work out. Why me?"

He shakes his head, and I'm not sure if I'm making things worse than they already are, but I want to understand the pattern of abuse and why some men get to this point.

"We weren't meant for each other, but that doesn't mean there isn't someone out there for that you'd be perfect with." I look at my legs, which are red from the rope rubbing against my ankles.

"I'll be in jail the rest of my life," Eli screams. "If I kill myself—"

"If you kill yourself, it's all over." I move my shoulders in an attempt to loosen the bonds around my wrists. "But you won't be in jail for the rest of your life. You can make this better."

"It wasn't supposed to end like this." Eli sits at the foot of the bed. "We were going to go away together. I had a place all set up. We were going to be happy."

"Where were we going to live?" I'm in the mind of a monster, and I shouldn't feel this calm, but my voice is steady.

Eli sighs. "North Dakota. On my family's land. There's a lake there, and we were going to live off the grid. At least for a while. With no distractions. It would have been perfect."

"We could still make that happen, Eli." I feed into his delusions. It's the only way to stay alive. "But it can't happen if we're both dead."

He looks at me, and I continue. "We need to answer the door. I'll tell them that we were here talking. That I want you to be here. That I invited you. That we're in love."

"You are lying," Eli screams back at me, and he flicks a tear that's fallen from his face.

I try to reach for his arm and then remember that my hands are tied together. "I'm not lying." I start to cry. "I don't want to die. And if you love me, you wouldn't hurt me. There's another way."

There's more pounding on the door, and someone speaks through what sounds like a megaphone. It's detective Rafferty. I recognize his voice.

"We need to go out together." I shift on the bed. "Together. And I'll tell them how much I love you."

Eli considers this. He puts his head in his hands and

sets the gun on the bed. It's so close to me. I remember all the times we were dating when I'd go to end things with him, and he'd threaten to kill himself. I never wanted that hanging over me, but in hindsight, it was one of the many weapons he used against me.

"What if I go out first?" I adjust the rope around my wrists. "You can untie me, and I'll talk to the detective. Tell him you're in here, and I invited you here."

"I can't trust you." Eli shakes his head and picks up his gun.

"You can. But you have to untie me first."

Eli ponders this. He stands up and looks down the hallway again, and there are shadows outside of every window.

"If they break through the door," I say. "They will kill you. Don't let it get to that. It's not too late to change."

Eli takes a deep breath and unties my legs first. I think about kicking him, but I want to build trust, and he's so much larger than me that there isn't much I can do. He then moves onto my wrists. I stand up, completely untied.

"I'm going to go through the front door. With my hands up."

Eli looks around my room and puts his gun on my nightstand. "And then they'll come in for you. We need to keep our stories straight. You came here because I asked you to. We're in love. You meant me no harm."

Eli nods, and I back out of the room, never taking my eyes off him. It's loud outside and sounds like the entire town came out for the show.

"Eli," I say quietly. "I love you."

The words aren't as vomit-inducing as I thought they'd be. I've never said those words to him, but I will say and do anything to stay alive. I'm choosing my life over Eli's. Today isn't my day. There is still so much I want to see, do, and experience. I can't have it end this way.

He stands in the hallway, and when I reach the front door, I turn my back on Eli for the first time. With my hands up, I walk out and am immediately pulled away by an officer.

"Eli's in the house." I point through the open door. "He has a gun."

The officers storm inside, and another brings me to a car and puts me in the backseat. There's a woman already there. She's older and takes my hand in hers.

"Hi, Jenna," she says. "I'm Megan. And I'm your victim advocate."

Her words fade into the background as I watch them take Eli out of the house in handcuffs. Our eyes meet, and he knows everything I said was a lie. I've been scared for so long, that I don't know how to feel any other way.

AFTER WHAT FEELS LIKE HOURS of giving statements, I'm finally released. I know one thing. I will never spend another night in that house again. My parents take me to their home, but everyone shows up and lingers, tiptoeing around me.

Jake, Camilla, and Signe are there, as well as Dax, Carrie, and Kylie. And Robby shows up too. My mom takes Kylie and Signe to the playroom, and we sit around. Even detective Rafferty shows up to let me know that Eli has been booked, and because of the immediate threat he poses, there will be no bail set, and his first hearing is in two days. The charges against him are piling up, and Rafferty wants the DA to bring attempted murder charges against him as well.

"I'm fine," I say, and everyone looks at me. The conversations have been hushed, and no one seems to know what to say. Although I'm the one who went through everything today, it feels like the only path forward is for me to comfort them.

"I'm going to get myself a drink." I stand and walk toward the kitchen.

Dax shoots up. "Let me get it for you."

"No." I wave him away. "I can get it myself."

The kitchen is empty, and I take a deep breath. I stand at the kitchen sink, looking out the window. I feel like I'm floating above my body, watching all of this play out, but not really experiencing it. Maybe I am dead. Is any of this real?

"Hey."

I look up to see Robby standing there. "Robby."

He closes the gap between us and wraps me in his arms. My body stiffens at his touch, and when he feels it, he releases me.

"I was so worried, Jenna." Robby pinches the bridge of his nose, but tears fall anyway. "I thought I was going to lose you."

He blows out a breath and digs his palms into his face to remove the wetness that's settled there. "What can I do for you?"

I look around. "I need to be with my family. There's a lot of processing. . ."

No more words come out. I want to be happy that Robby's here. I want to provide words of comfort, and that I didn't mean anything I said, but instead, I feel uncomfortable, and want to be in the room with all the people, and not standing in the kitchen alone with him.

"Let's get back to the group." Robby narrows his eyebrows but then follows me out of the room.

Chapter Thirty

Robby

DAMN NON-PROFITS. I GET OFF the phone with Khalif, the executive director of Teaching America, letting me know that they are now on a hiring freeze, and he doesn't expect it to last long, but in the meantime, they can't hire me.

Yes, it might fulfill me more than corporate America ever did, but it doesn't feel very stable either. It makes me wonder if leaving Goldman Sachs makes the most sense. They've promised me a job. I could return to Chicago right after Labor Day, move back into my sterile condo, pick up where I left off as an investment banker.

All of this sounds like the definition of insanity—doing the same thing, over and over, and expecting different results. I was never happy in Chicago. Not overall. There were nice moments there. I loved having Sunday brunch with my parents most weeks, and it was great being so close to the water. I had a few good friends there, but I haven't invested much in those relationships after one of those friends got engaged to my ex-girlfriend, Lilly.

It all felt like a rat race to get ahead and climb the

corporate ladder In hindsight, even my relationship with Lilly wasn't real. What I have with Jenna is real. Or it was real. It feels like I've already lost that. Something has changed between us.

Same job. Same city. It's not what I want.

I head to town to meet the regulars, Jake, Camilla, Dax, and Carrie. It's Jenna's last night at The Pool Hall, and we wanted to help her shut the place down. It feels good that that's the reason, and not because we're scared Eli might show up.

It takes a moment for my eyes to adjust to the darkness of the bar when I walk in—such a juxtaposition from the light outside. I blink and see Dax waving me over to the corner. It's packed in here tonight. I work my way to the back corner.

"Why's it so crazy in here tonight?" I look around. "Is there a meat raffle or something?"

Dax slams a beer down in front of me. "It's a naming contest. The entire town is invested in what this place is called."

Camilla shouts so we can hear the noise of people and music. "I never thought the name Pool Hall was very original."

"Hey guys," Jake stands. "I just saw a pool table open up. Who's in?"

Dax and Carrie say they'll play, and they walk to the back room with Jake, and I take a seat at our long table next to Camilla.

"Do you have an opinion on a name?" Camilla points to the bar, where there are three large glass jars, and I catch Jenna's eye. She waves at me.

"I may go up there soon and vote. How long do I have?"

"Until ten." Camilla glances at her watch, and then

holds her glass to mine. "Cheers bro."

"Cheers, Cam."

Jenna scrambles behind the bar, and I watch. She moves from customer to customer, taking orders, filling drinks, and wiping up spills. Camilla puts her arm on my elbow.

"What's the plan there, Robby?"

I turn and look at Camilla. I take a deep breath and a long sip. "There's no plan."

"No plan?" Camilla squints her eyes. "How do you feel about her?"

"I fucking love that girl."

She presses on. "Like you love all the Abrams? 'Oh, I fucking love the Abrams. They're like family.' Or you love her like, 'I can't live without her and want her to be the future mother to my children?'"

Camilla is animated, moves her hands around, and does voices as she describes these two very different types of love.

"Fine. You were right all along. We're sleeping together." As soon as the words come out of my mouth, Camilla pretends like she's going to vomit all over the table. "Well, we were at least."

She swats me on the shoulder. "Umm, duh."

My love for Jenna encompasses both loves that Camilla described. I've always loved Jenna. As a kid, I didn't have a word for it, but I felt like Jake, Dax, and Jenna were more than our friends. They felt like our extended family, so yes, I loved them. I loved Jenna two years ago, both because of familiarity and because she's the easiest person in the world to love.

"She leaves in two weeks." I look up as Jenna walks over to us. "And there has been no talk about the future. And something changed after what Eli did."

Camilla grabs my arm. "Are you going to tell her how you feel?"

"Hey, guys." Jenna reaches our table. "Sorry I haven't been over much yet. We got slammed."

She points toward the bar. "Are you going to vote on the new name for The Pool Hall?"

"I'll throw in my vote." I squint, trying to read the options. "What are the three finalists?"

Jenna stands between Camilla and me. "Okay, Madhouse on Main." She throws her arm out in both directions as if we could imagine how the sign would read.

"Then, there is The Wheaton Watering Hole."

"And third?" Camilla asks.

Jenna puts an arm around me and another around Camilla. "The Pool Hall."

There's an invisible barrier around Jenna that existed at the beginning of the summer and seems to be back.

"The Wheaton Watering Hole sounds accurate." I look at her.

"That's my vote, too," Camilla says.

"Okay," Jenna squeezes Camilla's shoulders. "I'm throwing two votes in the bowl for The Wheaton Watering Hole."

I stay well after everyone else leaves. I've gotten in the habit of picking her up, more out of protection, but now, it's because I want to maximize every moment I get with her. It's after midnight before Jenna shuts down the bar and locks it up for the last time.

"Can I give you a ride?" Jenna hesitates, but then nods.

"I'm happy to walk too," she says, but heads in the direction of my car parked out front.

We get in the car, and are silent for a couple of blocks, but then Jenna turns to me. "Have you heard anything from Teaching America yet?"

I shake my head. "They're on a hiring freeze. Everything's been delayed."

Her face crumples. "Robby. No."

"Yeah." I turn right down her parents' street. "I know."

Jenna continues to stare straight forward. "Now what?"

"Return to Chicago and wait."

"Is that what you want?" Jenna bites her lip, finally looking at me. "To go back to Chicago?"

"No." I say it almost in a whisper. "It's not what I want. But I've spent three months not earning a paycheck."

We arrive at her parents' house, and I turn the engine of the car off, and look at Jenna, but she avoids looking back at me. "You're welcome to come to the cottage."

"No," Jenna shakes her head. "I feel safe here, you know?"

I grip the steering wheel tighter. "I know."

She opens the door before I can consider saying anything else. "Thanks for the ride, Robby."

If Jenna asked me right now to follow her to New York, I wouldn't hesitate. I'd see if I could get a job at our Goldman's Office there until something else came. And if that didn't work out, I'd wait tables, work in a bookstore, or as a barista. But she's not asking me.

I don't feel I have the right to ask anything of Jenna. She finally has the opportunity to leave this nightmare behind and sparkle in the way she always should have been. Jenna has spent too much time sacrificing who she was and could become for everyone else; now it's her moment.

Chapter Thirty-One

Jenna

THE WOMEN GET READY AT Dax and Carrie's home, and the men at Jake's. Except for Malik, he's with us too. Carrie wanted today to be simple. Malik went and got ordained, and he's performing the ceremony, and then it's pretty much all family.

Carrie wears a beautiful white summer dress, and her mom, Juniper, adjusts a flower crown on her head. It feels good to be in the background instead of the center of attention. Ever since what happened, I've wanted to escape to a place where no one knows anything about me and my experiences. Yet, in a very short amount of time, anyone who reads *Harper's Bazaar* will know more about me than makes me comfortable. I was ready to be the face of domestic violence until I almost lost my life.

"Oh, Meadow, you look beautiful," her mom says, standing behind her and looking in the full-length mirror.

Carrie fixes the flower crown on Kylie's head and leans into her. "You look beautiful too, Kylie. Your dress is perfect."

Kylie giggles and spins. Her dress flies up as she spins. "Daddy is marrying Mommy Carrie today."

Juniper picks Kylie up and pulls her close. "No calling me Grandma, right?"

Kylie cups Juniper's face. "Nope. I'll call you Juniper. I promised."

There was much talk about how to honor Zari today, especially for Kylie. Dax and Carrie invited Zari's parents and sister, so they'll be here today too. And then they're going to take Kylie to Atlanta for a few nights, and the newlyweds are spending a few days at Carrie's B&B.

"Carrie, you do look fabulous." Malik wraps his arms around her. "Now, let's get our little Carrie married."

We take a few cars to Jake's. Dax and Carrie hired an event planner to come out and set up the space and then cater a dinner afterward. I see my parents, and I go and sit by them. There are only a few rows of chairs. My parents are here, and Jake and Camilla are standing up front as their witnesses, so I hold Signe. Malik officiates, and Robby shows up with Sunny and Sis on his arms.

Robby looks fancier than usual, which is saying something. His pants hit him at the ankle and are a light green color. When he sees me staring, he winks. And then Zari's parents, and Amina, her sister are the only other people here. It's a small group.

A single violinist plays as Dax walks down the aisle, holding hands with Kylie. There isn't a dry eye here, except mine. For some reason, I haven't been able to cry since that day. I've tried, but it almost feels as if something died in me.

Dax wipes away a tear and then nervously chuckles. We make eye contact, and I blow him a kiss. When Zari died, I couldn't have dreamed that he'd be happy again. Life is funny that way. It keeps moving forward even after we lose people. I'm glad that Dax found Carrie. She's an amazing friend, so wonderful to Kylie, and she makes my brother happier than. I hope I can find happiness like my brothers have, and it doesn't have to be in a romantic partner. I just want to be happy.

We all stand when Carrie walks down the aisle on Juniper's arm. She looks straight ahead at Dax and Kylie. She laughs too. She seems nervous at the attention, as that's never been her thing. Carrie and I are a lot of like. We've both experienced our fair share of life, and it changes a person, and teaches us how to compartmentalize our feelings instead of expressing them so outwardly.

Kylie stands for the entire ceremony, and when Carrie and Dax exchange rings, they include Kylie in the ceremony and give her a locket necklace. Amina does a reading. The entire thing only lasts about twenty minutes, but it was special and beautiful, and I'm happy I could be here. Being around all of these people is safe. I also can't wait to leave. Although once my article is published, everywhere I go, much of my story will be known to people. Well, the parts of my story I chose to tell.

There's one long table for all of us, and I see an empty chair next to where Robby sits. I go to sit down, but before I have a chance, Sunny takes Sis's hand and leads her to that chair. I find another empty one next to Camilla. Robby and I need to talk, but the timing never seems right.

Camilla turns to me. "How many days left?"

"Not that I'm counting." I fold a napkin onto my lap. "But a little over a week."

She lowers her voice. "How are you feeling these days?"

It's all anyone asks me. Everyone in town stares at me, whispers, and looks at me with pity. It's a lot of the reason I want to go. I am much more than a survivor, and no one needs to feel sorry for me.

"Ready to move on." When I say the words, Camilla squeezes my shoulder.

"Jake and I can't wait to see you in New York. You're

going to take it by storm." Camilla forks her salad.

"I can't wait to be there, settled in my new apartment." I haven't had four walls that belong to me in such a long time. I need the freedom that living alone will give me.

"I still can't believe you rented an apartment without seeing it." Camilla takes a sip of her drink. "You are so much braver than me."

"That's the way it's done these days." My eyes find Robby's from further down the table, and he smiles at me, but I look down.

"Excuse me." I push my chair out and stand, and head inside. I'm trying to be supportive to Dax and Carrie on this happy day, but I'm also not in the mood for this. I want to lie in bed and be paralyzed in my thoughts, like I've done every other night since.

I go inside to grab my purse and rest my elbow on the kitchen counter and take a few deep breaths. It's not long before Robby walks through the door. "Hey, there. I wanted to say goodnight before I left. It's time to get Sunny and Sis home." He points to the door.

"They lasted a while. That's good." I blow out a breath.

Robby keeps his hand on the doorknob and hesitates but then says. "I know this will be a busy week for you but let me know if you want to hang out at some point."

"Will do."

"I think about you constantly." Robby moves closer to me and leans back against a counter. "I can't imagine how things have been for you. And there is no pressure from me. But I want you to know that I'm here."

"Robby," I say his name slowly. I want to tell him that I'm not okay, and that ever since that day I've felt like I was drowning, and that part of me wanted to keep sinking to the bottom instead of being pulled out. I don't say those things.

"I'll call you." I force the corners of my lips to turn up in the semblance of a smile.

Robby's mouth falls open, but nothing comes out. He pushes off the counter. "Goodnight, Jenna."

Chapter Thirty-Two

Robby

JENNA HAS BEEN PULLING AWAY from me. It's gradual, but I feel it. We text less, talk less, and only see each other when I'm the one who reaches out. I don't blame her at all. I only wish it were different. Or I want the circumstances to be different. No matter how much I fight it, our lives continue to head in opposite directions. I miss the physicality of our relationship, but just as strongly, I miss talking to her.

There's a light knock at the cottage door, and I barely hear it. I rush to see Jenna standing on the other side.

"Hey." I pull her into a hug, craving her touch. "I didn't expect to see you tonight."

"Yeah." She walks in and looks around. "I couldn't sleep. I know you're nocturnal, and figured you'd still be up."

"You know me well." I walk to the kitchen and put water in the kettle. "I was doing nothing. Well, I was sitting at my computer and figuring out some future work stuff. But I'd much rather hang out with you."

The kettle cries out, and I fill our cups with steaming

hot water. I hand her the glass of tea bags to choose her flavor. She digs around and then pulls out peppermint.

I grab a bag of green tea, and go to sit on the couch, and Jenna follows. "Are you all ready to go?"

Jenna sits and then blows on the steaming water. "Almost."

She leans back on the couch and stares down at her hands.

"Is everything okay?" I finally ask.

She takes a sip of tea. "When I leave for New York, I think I need to leave for real."

Jenna runs a finger along the rim of her cup and looks at me. "This summer has been, well, it's been a lot."

I fold a leg over my other and lean my elbow on the back of the couch. "Are you okay?"

Jenna puts her cup on the coffee table and rubs her temples. "I thought I was. I wrote that article, submitted it and agreed to it being published with my real name. I felt invincible. Strong as fuck. But now. . ."

She puts her head between her hands and rubs her scalp. Her face is covered from my view. "But then everything. . ."

Her voice is so soft. She finally looks at me. "I'm not okay. I'm not even a little okay."

I reach my hand for hers, but when our fingers touch, I feel her body tense, and I pull back. I hate that my touch makes her scared. I'm supposed to be a source of comfort.

"What can I do for you, Jenna?" I blink away a tear. I can't fix this for her. I can't pull her to me and tell her everything will be okay and assure her that she's safe.

"You need to let me leave." Her eyes meet mine. "Not because I don't." She stops. "You're intertwined in all that happened this summer, and I need time and space from all of it. I'm so fucked up, Robby." She shakes her head, and her hair swishes in front of her face. "And I need to go figure out my shit without the constant reminders of this summer."

I gulp down the emotions that start in my chest and threaten to come out. "I understand. You don't have to explain. I get it. I do."

Jenna shakes her head. "I realize none of this is fair."

I bark a laugh, or maybe it's an escaped sob. I can't even tell at the moment. "Nothing that happened to you is fair. You deserved none of it."

I have no right to ask anything of Jenna, and I know that. I'm not even surprised that we're having this conversation. I felt it coming the moment Eli violated her in such a big way. There's a huge part of me that's relieved we're having it. Part of me thought Jenna would leave without giving me closure—without saying goodbye.

I know that we have love for each other, and if Eli and the trauma that ensued at his hands hadn't been part of this summer's story, we might be having a different conversation. All of that did happen, and it's changed Jenna. And I love her so much that I have no right to ask her to reconsider making me a part of her life.

"You get to call the shots here." I take a sip of my tepid tea. "And if you want to talk, call or text me. I'm always here. And if you want to see me, I'll be there. No questions asked. I'll give you the space you need. I promise you that."

I study Jenna, and her brightness is gone. She's still effortlessly breathtaking, but her spirit is damaged. "Thanks, Robby."

She gets up from the couch and looks back when she reaches the door. "I'm not leaving for a few days, but I wanted us to be on the same page."

"I'm on whatever page you're on," I assure her.

Because telling her that I'm in love with her, and forcing her to process one more thing, feels like the most selfish thing I could do right now. Instead, I let her go.

Chapter Thirty-Three

Jenna

In five days, I fly to New York City. There is no way I'd be crazy enough to bring a car there, so all I'm bringing is two large suitcases, and I'm shipping the rest. My mom is staying with me in the city for a few days, and she will help me furnish my apartment. Everyone has tried to book tickets to see me, but I ask for at least three months of settling in before I play host to anyone. I've also told my parents that I probably won't make it home for the holidays this year. I need time and space.

"Kylie." I throw her a towel so she can help me dry the dishes. "You know you'll always be my favorite oldest niece, right?"

Her brown eyes somehow get even bigger, and she runs to me and hugs me. "I'll never tell Signe that I'm your favorite."

I don't bother to correct her or tell her that she'll always be my oldest niece, and that's what I meant. Dax walks through the door.

"Hello." When Kylie hears her dad's voice, she runs to the door.

"Daddy, you're home." He picks her up.

"Were you good to Auntie Jenna?" He asks her.

"Yes. We made cookies."

Carrie then walks through the door. "Hey, guys."

I look at the clock hanging on the wall. "I should get going. I have about a billion things to do before I leave."

"Let me walk you out," Dax says.

I hug Carrie and say another goodbye to Kylie, and Dax follows me through the door.

Dax walks me to my car. This summer seemed like it passed in a blink of an eye while simultaneously feeling like I lived several lives.

"How are you feeling about leaving?" Dax looks at me and then wraps his arm in mine.

"Excited. Scared shitless." I rest my head on his shoulder. "You know, all the emotions one feels when moving to a city where one block has a bigger population than the entire town I live in now."

Dax laughs. A few minutes pass between us without words, but then he turns to me. "Are you and Robby going to continue seeing each other?"

I'm pretty sure Dax loves Robby almost as much as he loves me. But the sound of his name gives me a lump in my throat. "No."

Dax pulls his lips into a line. "I like how he treats you."

I like how he treats me too. And I like who I am around Robby. He's just good. So good, that sometimes I'm embarrassed that I spent two years of my life so angry at him. Although he didn't do everything perfectly, most guys I know would have slept with me and then mentioned that girlfriend back home. Not Robby. He's loyal.

"Our lives are not aligned right now. Maybe never." I say the words so quietly that Dax leans closer to hear me. And I'm damaged. But I don't say that. Dax doesn't have the ability to separate someone's pain from his own, so I spare him from how badly I'm doing. That I feel like I'm stuck beneath an elephant that refuses to get off me. I can't tell him any of this.

"So, you're going your separate ways?" We stand at my car, and I open the door. "And that's what you both want?"

"What we want?" I say back to him. "I haven't gotten what I want in a really long time, Dax. It's what I need, and Robby understands that."

THE NEXT COUPLE OF DAYS makes me wish I could escape the long goodbye and leave all of this behind me. Because every day, there's a new one to say. But I've saved the hardest goodbye for last. Robby. It feels impossible to walk away from all that he is to me. I asked him to stop by my parents' house to say goodbye. We've had our last goodbye sex. Then we had a goodbye conversation. And now's the hard part. Leaving.

He looks at my suitcases on the floor in my parents' entryway. "You're all packed?"

I look around. "Pretty much."

He tries his best to smile, but it's not a happy one. "Are you sure I can't drive you to Minneapolis? You know I'm happy to."

I shake my head. "My parents wanted to. You know how it is."

He nods. I don't tell him that goodbye at the airport would be too difficult. I want to wake up tomorrow and rip the band aid off instead of doing a three-hour car ride, with my heart breaking further with every word unsaid.

"You've come a long way, kid." Robby winks at me.

"My expectations were so low for the summer." I walk to my childhood room and double-check that I've packed everything. When I see I have, I flick off the light. "You were the best part of it. I hope you know that."

Robby then follows me into the kitchen, and his laughter fills the space. "You were mine too, Jenna."

I loop my hand through one of my suitcase handles. "I wish things were different."

Robby closes his eyes for a moment. "I'll never regret anything that happened between us this summer."

"Me neither." I reach up to his face and cup it because I need to feel near him one last time.

I gently kiss his cheek and am relieved when the touch doesn't make me want to hyperventilate. Ever since that day. That terrible day. I can't stand to be touched.

I want to tell him how much I wish things were different. That I wish I were different. Not this damaged girl, who let bad things happen to me. I want to ask him to wait for me, as long as it takes to come out the other side not sad and damaged. I can't ask that of him because I have no idea how long it will take until I feel like me again. Most days, I'm confident I'll never be the same.

Even though it's all true, what I said to him the other night is also true. I'm broken, and I need to heal from things and prove to myself that I can make it on my own. Maybe I'll never be whole again. Maybe none of us are complete, and we're all trudging through life doing the best we can with what we're given, but I know Robby deserves better than anything I could offer.

Robby wipes a tear from his cheek. "I'm proud of you, Jenna."

I close my eyes, and he's staring at me when I open

them back up. "I know you are."

My own tears threaten to drop, and I blink them back. "You'll always mean a lot to me."

Robby smiles. "Even with my ridiculous polo shirts."

"And your loafers," I add.

He steps toward me, but then stops himself. "Promise me you'll never poison Signe against me. We could be her favorite aunt and uncle if we play our cards right."

I wrap my arms so tightly around him. "Obviously, Robby. We are so much cooler than Dax and Carrie."

I need to leave, and I know I'm doing all of this for the right reasons, but it's still hard to say goodbye. Robby's grip around me tightens, and I press his hand against my chest and then kiss it. I slip out of his reach, but before I leave the kitchen, I turn to face him.

He follows me to my parents' entry way and looks in the direction of the living room. "I need to grab my parents, and we need to go."

Robby stands by the door and tucks his hands into the pockets of his shorts. He looks down, pinches the bridge of his nose, and then looks up at me. "I texted you Liam's number. He's expecting you to reach out when you get there. Only if you want to."

Liam. Robby and Camilla's cousin who lives out there. A really nice guy, but not Robby.

"Thanks."

Robby presses his lips together and nods. My stomach is in knots. The kind only lack of sleep, and painful goodbyes can give to me. It's a nauseating kind of pain, and I don't know how to get rid of it.

Neither of us moves or says anything. If this goodbye is necessary, why does it hurt this much?

"I really need to go," I say again, and Robby holds his arms out to me. I smell him one last time, and he puts his hand on the doorknob, ready to walk out.

"Robby," I say. "I need to ask you something?"

He looks at me and brushes my hair out of my face.

"Do you use dryer sheets? How do you always smell like you just walked out of one of those Bounce commercials?"

His chest shakes against me as he laughs. "I use two, Jenna. That's the trick."

I let myself rest against his chest for a moment longer and take deep breaths. I grab his ball cap, take it off him, and run my fingers through his already tousled hair.

"Jenna." Robby puts a hand on my shoulder and the other on my waist. He takes a deep breath, closes his eyes, and then opens them. They're red-rimmed, probably from being tired, and he rapidly blinks. "I'm always here for you. Always."

I nod. Because if I talk, my voice will betray me.

"You go to New York and kick ass. Don't let anyone get in your way."

I smile and put my head against his chest because I can't handle looking into his eyes.

He kisses the top of my head. "Go build the life you've always wanted, the life you deserve."

"And you?" I don't lift my head when I say the words.

Robby takes my chin and lifts it. He kisses me lightly on the lips. "Wherever you are, I'll always be your biggest fan."

One more hug and this one feels like goodbye. I hand Robby his cap back, but he takes it and puts it on my head. It's his favorite Chicago Bulls cap. I rub the spot after he kisses my cheek.

He takes a step back, opens the door, and steps outside. "Keep blowing shit up, Jenna Abram. The world is going to be a better place because of you."

I smile, a tight-lipped, get me the hell out of here before I fall apart kind of smile. Robby closes the door slowly between us, and I'm hoping the worst of the pain is over.

Chapter Thirty-Four

Robby

JENNA'S BEEN GONE FOR SIX days. All of which I've slept in town at Sunny and Sis's because the moment she left, I vacated the cottage. I couldn't stay there. The memories were like ghosts haunting me. She hasn't called, nor have I. She needs to determine where, if anywhere, we go next. I need to let her go.

Everyone is coming to Wheaton for Labor Day weekend to move Sunny, and Sis into Pelican Crest Assisted Living officially. My uncle Larry, aunt Diane, and cousin David are all flying in from Florida. Their other son, Liam, will be arriving shortly from New York, and my parents are coming in from Chicago. It's good I vacated the cottage anyway, as it provides them more room to stay.

"Robby, will you help with the photos?" Camilla points to all the pictures that line the dining room wall.

I start taking them down and piling them into a box. These photos convey many memories of the four grandchildren growing up through the ages. All of our school pictures going back to preschool: my dad and his brother Larry as kids, with a much younger Sunny and

Sis.

"How's it going, Robby?" I turn and watch Sunny shuffle into the room. This house is being transformed into nothing but four walls as we remove all the memories.

"We're here." Everyone comes barreling through the door. They all had flights landing at similar times in Minneapolis, and they rented a large SUV.

I hug my parents, aunt, uncle, and cousins. My mom organizes us. "How about we divide and conquer? Kids, you start upstairs in the bedrooms, and the grown-ups will keep moving down here."

Yes, almost thirty-year-old me is still a kid in her eyes. I head upstairs with Camilla, Liam, and David. Instead of dividing and conquering, we all start in what we affectionately call the green room.

Liam reaches into his bag, pulls out a magazine, and hands it to me. "I thought you'd want to see this. I picked it up at an airport gift shop."

It's Jenna. On the fucking cover. Everyone crowds around me, but Liam pulls out more from his bag.

"I bought a few."

The cover is gorgeous. It looks like the photo was taken in a studio, but I know it was taken at Jake and Camilla's. She sits on a stool, and her head rests on her wrist. Her countenance is serious. She looks like any other celebrity you'd see in this magazine. Jenna's world is about to change. It's going to grow and become even better, and this summer we spent together will quickly become a distant memory.

"You know." Liam puts his hand on my shoulder, bringing me back to reality. "She and I had drinks a couple of nights ago."

"Oh good." I somehow manage to choke the words out. "I was hoping you guys would connect."

Camilla sits on the bed, rifling through the magazine. She looks up. "How'd Jenna seem?"

"Great." Liam sits on the bed next to Camilla. "It turns out we don't live far from each other at all, so I'm going to introduce her to some of my friends. I'm having a party next weekend, and she's going to come. It can be hard to meet people in the city."

Camilla's eyes meet mine. They're probing like she will find some long-lost answer in them. I shake my head. I can't do this right now. I can't think about this. In my head, I think of all the worst scenarios. What if Liam falls for her too? And then they date. I try to remove these thoughts from my head. I want Jenna to be happy. She deserves it, no matter what that looks like for her.

"Look in here." David points to the large walk-in closet, and we all huddle around the doorway.

There's a large bin of all the clothes we used to play dress-up in. When we were little, Camilla always had Liam, David, and I wrapped around her finger and would have us all dress as princesses.

I pick up the dress I always got to wear. It was just an old, white slip of Grandma Sis's, but it was my favorite. Camilla grabs a tissue from the top of the dresser, and I hadn't even realized that she had started crying. Then she hands it to me. It's me that's crying. My cheeks are soaked.

"Sorry guys." I dab my eyes. "This is harder than I thought it would be."

"I dreaded coming here." David digs his palms into his eyes.

Liam nods. "I can't imagine driving by this house on Main Street when we visit and seeing another family in this house. How can this house be anyone but Grandpa and Grandma's?"

"Let's go." My dad yells from downstairs. "We're

ready to drive over to Pelican Crest."

We all look at each other and head toward the door. I pause and look at the room one more time, as more stuff gets hauled outside.

When I get downstairs, Jake is waiting with Signe attached to his chest. "This pile here is the last of it." He glances at us all. Now, all our eyes are red.

We all drive separately to Pelican Crest, which is only a few blocks away. I help Jake, Liam, and David carry heavier items from the trailer. There isn't much. Camilla helps Sunny and Sis get inside.

Apartment 2B. We open the door, and it's sterile. The floors are large, white, porcelain tiles that make this place look more like a hospital than an apartment. The kitchen doesn't have an oven, but it has a cooktop surface, which will be good for Grandma Sis to make her tea. There's a short hallway with one bedroom, and across from that, a bathroom, with handicap railings everywhere. My mom and Aunt Diane start putting clothes away in the dresser we just carried in. Jake and I put out their two blue chairs in the living room. My dad works on getting the TV set up.

"This is going to be a great place to live." Sunny plops down in his chair.

Sis sits too and looks around. There isn't much to see. The view from their window is a small courtyard and more rooms of Pelican Crest.

Everything is moved into the place in less than thirty minutes. I stand in the kitchen with Camilla next to me. The tears won't stop. How does someone's full life of over eighty years get reduced to a five-hundred square foot apartment? Sunny and Sis spent their lives traveling, working, and building community. They raised two sons, have grandchildren, and a great-grandchild. And now they sit in this sterile little apartment, in their two blue chairs, as my mom and aunt hang pictures up, trying to make it feel like home.

But this isn't home.

"At least they're together," Camilla whispers as she wraps her arms in mine. It's like she read my mind.

"How can we do this to them?" I choke out. "After everything they've done for us, it feels like we're confining them to prison. Or death."

Camilla takes my hand and leads me outside. We walk down the long hallway until we reach a door. The door opens to the courtyard. Camilla sits on a bench, and I follow.

"I had to get you out of there." Camilla squeezes my arm. "You were bringing the room down."

I look at her, and she's crying too. Camilla never cries. That's always been my role. I've always felt things deeply, and it's something I've often hated about myself.

She rests her head on my shoulder. "Liam knows that you and Jenna, I don't know, had or have a thing."

"Okay." I sit up straighter.

"Thought you should know." Camilla lifts her head off me. "Because I know your brain, and I could see it spinning."

"Well. Jenna isn't mine." I glance at Camilla. "And I want her to be happy. She deserves to be happy."

"Damn it, Robby. You're infuriating."

I glance at Camilla, who turns red and looks mad.

"I've been sitting back, we all have, waiting for you to figure out your shit, and you just let her go."

"Camilla," I say. "Jenna had to go. Too much happened."

"I know. But she didn't have to go without you telling her how you feel."

"I almost did." I shake my head. "But after everything

happened with Eli, something changed in her. It would have felt so self-serving to share how I'm feeling and ask her to love me back."

Jenna always acts like she's fine, and I know she does it for everyone else's benefit. I could tell she wasn't fine. And as much as I miss her, I also hope she's finding what she needs to heal from her trauma.

"I didn't realize Jenna was struggling so much." Camilla loops her arm in mine.

I LAND IN CHICAGO ON a Tuesday morning, and around noon, my phone rings.

"Hey man, It's Khalif from Teaching America. Is this a good time?"

"It's a great time," I say quickly, because I've been waiting for this call.

"The hiring freeze is over. If you're still interested, we'd love to bring you on board."

"Yes," I say without giving it any thought, because this is all I've hoped for all summer."

"Great. We have openings in two cities. Los Angeles, Or New York. Why don't you give it some thought—"

"New York," I say, and Khalif laughs into the phone. It barely feels like a choice. I was always planning on New York, with or without Jenna.

"It's a good choice. I'll have my assistant send over the paperwork this afternoon. See you in New York, Robby."

The condo association in my building gives me the green light to rent it out. It's already paid off, and I'd rather have the monthly income coming in than sell it outright. I don't have a lot of furniture, but I decide to rent it fully furnished. I'd rather start over in New York than bring these things with me. I have twenty-five applicants on the first day I listed it but chose a newlywed couple from Minnesota who moved to Chicago for their careers. They seemed like good people.

I found an apartment in New York online and put down six months of rent. It's nestled between Hell's Kitchen and Lincoln Square, It has views of the Hudson River from the large windows in the apartment.

I start with Teaching America on October first, which means I have less than three weeks to settle everything and move into my new place.

There's been zero communication with Jenna in almost two weeks. No text, calls, or anything, and although Camilla's advice hangs out there, I don't want to be disruptive. Jenna and the *Harper's Bazaar* article have been discussed by every news outlet since the magazine came out, and I have a sneaking suspicion that she's not the same person she once was. It isn't always the passage of time that changes us. It's the things that happen to us.

Chapter Thirty-Five

Jenna

THE SUN SHINES THROUGH THE window of the coffee shop as I wait for Gabby to show up. It's a warm September day, and it's been two weeks since the article came out. Although I'll never get used to walking by a newsstand and seeing my face, it's easy to remain undiscovered in New York.

That's probably why so many celebrities choose to live here over Los Angeles. Everyone you meet is interesting, and everyone has a backstory. People roam the streets mainly unbothered. I like to put my long hair in a ponytail and throw on Robby's hat, and that's how I go out, and no one has stopped me once.

"Sorry, I'm late." Gabby sits down, her warm coffee in hand. "I hope you haven't been waiting long."

"Not at all." I smile and lean forward. "Plus, the people-watching in this city is amazing."

She laughs. "You have no idea. I could sit on a bench all day, watching the city move around me."

Gabby crosses her legs and puts on her business face. "How have things been for you? I can't tell you all the feedback we've gotten on the article. Our communications department gets several messages a day asking for you. People want you to be on their talk shows."

"I'm happy the article was received well." I lean back in my chair, holding my cup to my lips. "But I don't want to become famous for this. That was never my goal."

"It might not have been your goal, but it's taken on a life of its own."

Gabby isn't wrong. Agents have contacted the magazine asking to represent me. My face is everywhere. The weirdest thing I've ever seen was the other day when I was walking through Times Square and saw my face on a giant billboard. My face. Jenna Abram. From Wheaton, Minnesota. It was a surreal moment.

"Imagine how much you could continue highlighting the issue." Gabby taps a finger on the table. "Or." Gabby's voice trails off, but then she starts again. "You could write a column for us monthly. It wouldn't be a feature, but it pays, and you could continue highlighting this important issue."

I've known since arriving in New York a month ago that I'd need to find a job here. I considered becoming a server or bartender, as I have a lot of experience with that, but now that my face is out there, I want the attention to cool down before I put myself out there.

My goal in being here, and starting school, is to be a journalist. This is a way I could make that happen.

"Gabby." I pull my lips into my mouth. "If you're serious, I'd really like to consider this. I could focus on all the letters I've gotten from domestic abuse survivors."

"That's all I'm asking." She smacks the table with her open hand. "And think about the other stuff. Exposure isn't always a bad thing."

Gabby leans forward and lowers her voice. "And we'd love a follow-up to the article if you're willing to open up about Eli and him coming to your house and the hearing."

I nod. It's something I've thought a lot about. It's something I've also talked to my therapist about at length.

"I'd want to think about that more, but I'd consider it."

She stands and turns to me before leaving. "I'll see you at the rooftop party this weekend, right?"

"I'll be there."

IT'S A PERFECT FALL DAY in New York, and from coffee, I head to my therapy appointment. I found a great one, and it's helping more than I realized therapy could. She specializes in trauma and PTSD. When I arrive at her fortieth-floor office, she's standing and waiting for me.

"Hey, Julie," I say, and she waves me in.

"Happy day to you, Jenna."

I sit on the couch, put a pillow over my lap, and reach over and grab one of her mints.

"How's your week going so far?" Julie grabs a notebook from her desk and moves it to her lap.

"Good." I grab another pillow and prop it behind my back. "I had coffee this morning with a friend from *Harper's Bazaar*. She offered me a column and an opportunity to tell more of my story."

Julie leans forward in her chair. "How would that make you feel? Telling more of your story."

I close my eyes and exhale in an even stream. "I like telling my story. I like being out front and center. What is wrong with me? I thought I was coming to New York to escape, but I'm actually contemplating becoming more public."

Julie shakes her head. "There is no should when it comes to healing. What's right for someone else might not be right for you."

"Telling my story makes me feel like I am taking my power back." I pop another mint in. "I thought I'd come to New York and be scared, looking over my shoulder. I was terrified I'd allow Eli to live rent-free in my head."

"And how do you feel?" Julie probes.

"Safe." I shake my head. "And confident that Eli will spend many years in jail and that my victim impact statement is a large part of that. I feel strong."

She smiles. "These are all good things to feel."

"They are," I admit. "But a man held me hostage in my home and threatened to kill me. Why do I feel this good so soon?"

Julie adjusts her chair and then puts her notebook down. "There is no good reason some people can move on in healthy ways from trauma and others can't. But you have many positive things in your life that are helping you along. One, you sought therapy. Two, you have a support system in your family and friends that most people could only dream of."

"And three," Julie continues. "You have a platform to elevate your voice and the voice of others who have experienced something similar. There is power in that, Jenna. And maybe not everyone wants that, but you've highlighted this issue."

"Are you telling me it's okay to feel as good as I do right now?"

Julie smiles. "It's okay to feel however you're feeling."

I rub my temples. "But why did I give up everything that made me happy? I felt like I deserved to feel pain. If something gave me joy, I ran. I said goodbye to. . ."

Robby's face comes into view. I walked away from

him. I didn't give our relationship a chance because I thought I didn't deserve happiness. At least not that soon. I thought people would expect me to be in mourning after such a traumatic event.

Julie presses her lips together. "I'm telling you that healing is not and will never be linear. I'm happy you feel as good as you do right now, but something might trigger you in the future, and you'll take a step back. What I am telling you is there is no right or wrong. You're exactly where you're supposed to be."

Julie looks at her clock, and then I do the same. Our hour is up. Our time together always goes by fast.

"Jenna." Julie stands. "Sometimes when we go through something as big as what happened to you, we convince ourselves that we don't deserve any better. So instead of waiting for something else bad to happen, we walk away from joy. From people. From happiness. But it's never too late to come to the realization that you didn't deserve what happened, and you do deserve all the good things."

I stand and let every word of hers penetrate my soul. Julie then walks to the door. "Same time, same place next week?"

"I'll be here."

Before she opens the door, she looks at me. "You're doing great, Jenna. Your life does not need to be defined by something that happened to you. You are much more than that."

I nod. "See you next time."

The elevator down is long, and I close my eyes and take deep breaths. When I get to the main floor, I walk into the autumn sun, grateful for where I'm at and how far I've come in such a short amount of time. Eli didn't have the power to take any of that from me.

Chapter Thirty-Six

Robby

I'VE BEEN IN NEW YORK for three months. It's early December, and I have never been more confident that I'm where I'm supposed to be. I teach three days a week at the largest school district in the country, the New York City School district. I commute to Queens these days and teach at an overpopulated and underfunded school. On the two days I don't teach, I do board work with Teaching America. This involves a lot of fundraising, awareness campaigns, and deployment initiatives across the largest school districts in the country.

The board work is all done via calls because Teaching America is in Chicago. On the days I'm in the classroom, I teach finance, which was never a class offering before. I'm also looking into starting a finance club. I go home every night knowing that I made a difference. That's something I never felt before.

I've slowly moved into my Lincoln Square apartment. It already has more personality than my Chicago condo ever had. I hung some of my favorite art on the walls and even had some frames of family. Mostly of Signe. I pulled out the pictures that Jenna and I took a couple of years ago in a Navy Pier booth and tucked that photo into my mirror in my bedroom. My favorite painting was gifted to me by a client when I did my stint in London. It's a Banksy, called *Girl with Balloon*.

Jenna may or may not know I'm in New York. If she knows, it's not because I've talked to her. We haven't communicated except for a few texts sent back and forth in early autumn. And I've told Camilla not to mention it to her because I want to respect Jenna's space. But I think of her constantly and hope she's settled and happy. I can't escape Jenna, though. She's everywhere. I walk by her photo at the Time Square magazine stands, and yesterday, I saw her photo from the *Harper's Bazaar* story on a bus. An actual city bus, with Jenna's face. I smiled so big when I saw it.

She's blowing shit up in the best way possible. Like I hoped she would. When I think of her, I imagine her going to fancy parties with famous people, sipping on expensive wine, and charming the pants off of everyone lucky enough to meet her. Jenna has arrived.

Camilla has talked to her and tells me she's doing well, but I purposely don't ask many questions, and Camilla deliberately doesn't offer much. Jenna needed a fresh start to heal and prove she could make it alone. I love her and will gladly give her that opportunity without getting in the way.

Tonight, Khalif is in town, and we're hosting a fundraiser dinner downtown for Teaching America. I take the subway and meet Khalif and others at the restaurant.

"There you are," Khalif says when he sees me. "The drinks and appetizers are being served, and once everyone has a beverage in hand, we can start with our talk."

I reach into my bag and grab marketing material that was sent to me from our Chicago office. I lay it out on the tables.

Khalif helps me set everything up. "I talked to Principal Johnson this morning. He said there is a ton of interest in the Finance Club. That's amazing."

"Yeah." I nod. "I actually talked to a buddy at Goldman Sachs, and I'm bringing over a group next week to visit the office, and then we'll go see the ringing of the bell when the market opens."

"Dude," Khalif says. "I can't tell you how happy I am to have you on board. And in New York, where you can tap into some of the people you know on Wall Street."

Our fundraising is largely a grassroots effort at this point. We have a few large donors that sustain us, but it's about people understanding who we are and what we do. It's about people understanding the history and the decisions based on underprivileged communities that led us to where we are today. Khalif tells the story of our public-school systems and neighborhood gentrification, the haves and have-nots, better than I've ever heard the story told. The money is very average, but the work fuels my soul, and I made enough in my previous life to be doing well financially. Renting my Chicago condo doesn't hurt.

AFTER THE EVENT, I HEAD uptown, where I'm meeting Liam and his buddy at a bar to watch a basketball game. I don't know when or if I'll ever feel like a New Yorker, but most of the time I know what train to grab, and how to get around.

"Hey, buddy." I put my hand on Liam's shoulder. He's already seated at the bar, and the game is on the big screen.

"It's great to see you, Robby," Liam says, and I order a Manhattan from the server.

His friend sits beside him. "Robby, this is Joe. Joe,

257

Robby."

The New York Knicks stomp on the Chicago Bulls, and we barely watch.

"I saw Jenna recently." Liam turns to me. "Does she know you're here?"

"Not sure." I take a sip of my drink. "Only if someone has mentioned it to her. But we haven't spoken."

"She looks good, man." Liam turns away from me to watch the Knicks's add to their lead against my Bulls. "I guess she's got a column now for the magazine."

I smile. I'm not surprised. Jenna will start at the Columbia School of Journalism in early January with an enviable resume. She was always going places.

The game ends, and we all go our separate ways, and I walk a few blocks to get the train heading uptown. The night is dark, but the city is lit up. People walk by in every direction, and some spill out of bars and restaurants on my route. And then I see her.

Jenna walks out of a building with a green overhanging sign that displays the name of the venue. Her long hair hangs straight down her back, and she wears black boots that come over her knees, and a short black dress. I pause and stare. A few people walk out after Jenna, and a man takes a coat he holds and places it over her shoulders. She turns over her shoulder to smile at him.

My feet feel riveted to the sidewalk, but I manage to move. Tucking myself into another building entrance, I hide from her, just in case she happened to look in my direction. Jenna hugs one of the women in the group, and then another, and those two women walk in my direction. Jenna waits at the curb with the man, and she laughs at something he says. A moment later, a black car pulls up in front of them, and the man holds the door open for Jenna, slides in himself, and then shuts the door.

When Jenna and I parted at the end of the summer,

all I wanted was for her to find happiness. I always hoped that I would find a way into Jenna's life and be part of all the joy she deserves, but I also knew there was a possibility that things wouldn't play out that way.

The car pulls away and I begin my walk again. I tuck my hands into my pockets and am happy that Jenna seems to be doing well, but also pretty damn devastated. Because there doesn't seem to be a reality that exists where I'm in Jenna's life, and she loves me the way I love her.

Chapter Thirty-Seven

Jenna

I DON'T HAVE AN ACTUAL DESK at the corporate headquarters of *Harper's Bazaar*, but Gabby and the team let me sit at one when I want to come into the office to work on my column. There is so much excitement, and I have the opportunity to see how magazines operate.

My column will probably only be short term. I aim to get into documentary storytelling, which I'll study at Columbia. I often think about my therapist Julie and her words to me. I have a platform to tell people's stories, more than only my own. That's what I want to do. Give a voice to the voiceless.

I decide to forego the subway and walk uptown toward my home. It's not a short walk, but it's a good way to learn the city. I cut over to Central Park, bask in the sun peeking through the trees, and marvel that a city this size can have such a large grassy space. When Kylie and Signe visit me, this will be the first place I bring them. I find a bench to sit and watch people walk by. I make up stories in my head about what their backstories are. Are they from here? Or are they from a small town like me, running from or to something new? Something better.

As people pass me by, I often wonder if anyone is actually from New York or are we all transplants. A microcosm of different races and cultures of people all brought together to live in this one place—an experiment.

And then I see him. Robby. He bites into a baguette, juggles it in one hand, and sips coffee from his other. He looks like he belongs here. His dark hair is pushed back, and his fitted button-down shirt is tucked into his pants.

I'm so surprised to see him that I almost convince myself that it can't be him. I didn't know he was here. I talk to my family back home constantly, but I don't bring up Robby, so neither do they. At least five times a day, I start a text to him and then erase it. I asked for space, and only partly because I needed it, but also, I was scared if I didn't say it first, then Robby would have the conversation with me. He'd tell me long distance romances don't work, and that there was only a small chance he'd end up in New York City. I was always scared of losing Robby, so I lost him on my terms. People who experience trauma shouldn't be allowed to make life-altering decisions for a certain amount of time.

Instead of walking by, he sits on a bench by a large tree. Not much separates us except a walking path and a bike path. He puts his coffee down on the bench and grabs his phone out of his pocket. He looks so handsome, and his face now cleanly shaven which gives him a boyish look. I want to walk over to him and say all the things I've left unsaid all the things. But instead, I pull out my phone and send him a text.

"Long time no talk. How are things in Chicago?" I hit send and wait for his reaction.

His lips turn up in a smile. I don't know what I would have done had he left me unread.

"Hey, stranger." His text says. "I was beginning to think you got all famous and forgot about your friends back home."

"Forget you? Unlikely, Robby Bergland."

He smiles again, and then I receive my next message. "Sorry, I've been quiet. I wanted to give you space to figure out your new life. I didn't want to suffocate you."

"Have you moved on from your preppy look to something more casual?" I hit send.

Robby laughs, and our benches are close enough together that I can hear the beautiful sound escape him. "Totally, Jenna. Now I favor joggers and t-shirts. That's all I wear anymore. You wouldn't even recognize me."

I press my lips together and smile. He's, of course, lying.

"Hmm." I text. "Because from here, it looks like you're wearing a designer tweed coat with orange, sorry, salmon khakis."

As soon as I hit send, Robby's face jerks in one direction and then the other, and then his eyes meet mine, and it takes him a moment to realize it's me. His Chicago Bulls cap is low on my head, and my hair is in a side braid.

We both stand and walk toward each other. He continues to look at me in disbelief.

"Holy shit, Jenna." Robby smiles. "What are you doing here?"

"What am I doing here?" I point to myself. "I live here. What are you doing here?"

"I live here too." He nods to the bench he was just sitting on, and we both take a seat. "I have an apartment. In Lincoln Square. Not far from here."

I lean my elbow on the bench and study him. "You live in New York? We live in the same city? How long have you been here?"

Robby takes a sip of his coffee. "Three months. I moved in late September."

"And you didn't think to tell me this big news?"

Light snow begins to fall, and he pops the collar on his tweet coat.

Robby adjusts his body to more fully face me. The snow catches on his coat "I wanted to give you space." Robby's voice trails off, but he studies me with such intensity, that my body heats up a few degrees.

"Jenna." I've missed the sound of my name coming out of his mouth. "I was going to reach out but wanted to . . ."

He looks down at the space between us. "I didn't want to disrupt what you have going for you here." He pulls the bill of my cap.

"You got a job with Teaching America?"

He smiles. "I did. Shortly after you left, I chose between New York and Los Angeles. Easy decision."

"The easiest." I smile.

"My polos wouldn't have the same effect in the southern California heat." Robby winks at me.

"It's," I stutter. "It's really good to see you, Robby Bergland."

"New York looks good on you." Robby looks at me, mouth a little open. "You seem really happy."

I notice the contrast of the snow on his dark hair, and the way his cheeks are a little pink from the coolness outside. I observe the way his lip twitches a little, and he stops it by pulling his bottom lip into his mouth.

"Things have fallen into place here." I pull at my braid.

Robby's lips turn up in a smile. "I saw you the other night. Downtown. Coming out of some sort of event, all dressed up."

My mouth falls open. "Why didn't you say hi?"

Robby looks down, and then he slowly raises his gaze

to me. "You were with someone. It looked like a date, and I didn't want—"

"It wasn't a date." The words spill out of me faster than intended. "They were colleagues from the magazine. We shared a car."

My phone buzzes, and I look down. It's George, my advisor at Columbia. He invited me to come in today to meet some faculty members over lunch. I need to run home and change before meeting him on campus.

"I'm sorry." I stand. "I'm running late for a meeting. I should go."

Robby stands too. "Yeah, I should get going too."

When I realize that I still have his cap, I take it off and try to hand it to him, but he shakes his head and leans in to whisper.

"You're famous now. I think you need that cap more than me."

I don't want to walk away, but I have to go. "It was great to see you."

"You too."

Robby puts his hands in his coat pockets but doesn't move. I smile one last time and walk in the other direction, knowing that if I'm going to get to my appointment on time, I should find the closest subway stop to get to my neighborhood.

"Hey Jenna," Robby catches up and wraps his fingers around my wrist.

"Yeah?" I turn to him, and he seems out of breath.

"Do you have plans this weekend?"

The rooftop party that Gabby invited to me, I think. But that's Saturday night.

Before I can respond, Robby pulls his coat tight. "If it's too soon, and you don't want to, or if you don't want to because you don't want to with me. Or if you're busy, honestly, it's—"

"Robby," I begin to say.

But at the same time, he says, "It's just really fucking great to see you."

My face flushes. "I'm free Friday night." Hope fills my chest cavity that once had housed a broken heart.

Robby looks at the ground and kicks an imaginary pebble. His eyes flicker up to mine. "I'd love to take you on a date."

"Ahh," I start, but Robby cuts me off.

"I mean, if you'd like to go on a date with me, I'd like to take you on one. Only if you want, of course."

Robby's face is red, and heat creeps up on my body. I've never seen Robby so unsure of himself, and it makes me want to wrap my arms around him.

"Yeah." Robby's body relaxes at my words. "I'd love that."

His smile reaches his eyes. "Great, I'll text you the details."

"Robby," I say, and he steps closer. "I really do have to go."

We both laugh, an awkward release of whatever we're feeling. "Of course. Bye Jenna. See you soon."

I walk away, and when I get a few steps, I turn over my right shoulder, and he's still standing there, hands in his pocket, smiling.

Chapter Thirty-Eight

Robby

JENNA GAVE ME HER ADDRESS after I insisted on picking her up at her apartment. I take a car service to her place, and it's not that far from my Lincoln Square apartment. After checking in with the doorman, I wait for Jenna to come down. I love that she found a building with a doorman.

"Hey." Jenna gets out of the elevator and waves me through the doorman. I hand her flowers.

"You didn't have to bring me flowers." Jenna pushes floor five, and she glances at me. "And you didn't have to go out of your way to pick me up."

The elevator door opens, and I hold it for her and follow her down the hallway, and she unlocks the door to her apartment.

"Well," I say, looking around her place. "It is our first date. I wanted to impress you."

Jenna opens a cupboard but turns to smile. "You took me on a date in Chicago, didn't you?"

She fills a vase with water, then sets it on a counter, unwraps the plastic around the flowers, and puts them in the vase.

"Technically, I had a girlfriend when we went to dinner in Chicago, so as far as I'm concerned, this is our first date."

"The girlfriend," Jenna says as she squeezes her eyes shut. "Don't remind me."

We stand, looking at each other, trying to make up for lost time. I've missed seeing Jenna, talking, and just being.

Jenna points behind her. "Tour?"

"Yes."

She claps her hands together. "It won't take long. My place isn't very big."

We start in the kitchen, which is cut off by a bar with stools, and then opens up to the living room. The wood floors are in perfect condition, and French glass doors lead to her bedroom. It's small, but it fits a bed and a dresser, and one entire wall of her bedroom is storage.

"And finally, the bathroom. Tour over."

Jenna standing in her new apartment, almost takes my breath away. She looks around proud, and she should be. I beam at her.

"You did it, Jenna. Your place is beautiful."

We walk out of her place. "Are you okay to walk? It's about a mile away."

"Yes," Jenna says right away. "Walking is perfect."

Side by side, we head in the direction of the restaurant, one I've wanted to try on the upper west side, which got really good reviews. Jenna and I make small talk, and the city moves around us. I remember when Jenna visited me for a long weekend in Chicago two summers back.

This Jenna is different. She looks like she belongs here. Some people stare in her direction, and I know it's because they know they've seen her somewhere.

I put my hand on the small of her back and lead her into the restaurant, and we take a seat in the back. The ambiance is beautiful. One wall is all brick, dimly lit, with a small candle in the center of the table.

Jenna looks around. "You're so fancy, Robby."

She wets her lips and takes a sip of the water the server brings by. "You know me, Jenna. I've always liked the finer things in life."

The menu looks great. Jenna wrinkles her brow as she studies it. "Thanks for asking me out."

"Thanks for saying yes."

Jenna puts her menu down and folds her hands on the table. "I can't miss the opportunity now that we're in the same city."

"Jenna," I say her name slowly, glancing at her from above my menu. Before I have a chance to say more, our server comes.

Our entire dinner is great. The food is amazing, and the conversation flows. We don't talk about anything serious, but she fills me in on the opportunity to write for *Harper's Bazaar*, the Columbia campus, and her budding friendship with Gabby.

I tell Jenna about Teaching America, the school I was assigned to, and how I want to create finance programs for underserved populations to teach the fundamentals of running a budget, whether at home or professionally.

"Do you want to continue walking?" I ask Jenna as we get outside the restaurant.

"Yes." She looks at me, and we cross the street toward Central Park. "I need to work off all the food I ate. And it's so mild out right now."

"I talked to Sunny and Sis today." I look at her and smile. "Sounds like the town will create a Jenna Abram day in your honor."

She covers her face with her hands and shakes her head. "Yeah, Dax called me earlier to give me crap about it. But let's be honest, he's jealous."

"He should be." I bark a laugh. "There's Jake Abram day. Now there's going to be a Jenna Abram day."

"Damn middle child problems." Jenna laughs. "Poor Dax."

We reach the park, and I don't know our destination, but we walk along the path, and I see a beautiful bridge in the distance, so we go toward that.

"Have you had any celebrity crushes slide into your DM's?" I nudge her on the elbow.

"No." Jenna rubs her arms over her sweater. "And I was so hoping Chris Evans would reach out."

"I had you more of a Chris Hemsworth kind of person." I take my cardigan off and put it around Jenna's shoulders.

She pulls it up to her face, smells the sweater, and lets out a long sigh.

"Enjoying my dryer sheets?" Jenna leans against the cast iron railing, and we step closer as a horse-drawn carriage goes by with two passengers in the back.

She laughs. "It smells so good. How do you always smell so good?"

Jenna turns to face me, and I put my hand next to hers, and we both grip the railing.

"Jenna, I …" My mouth and my brain are disconnected. I contemplate never telling her how I feel. Because if she doesn't feel the same way or want the same things, my hope will be gone instantly. There's finality in knowing.

Jenna puts her hand on mine and grins. "Is this the part of the date where you tell me that because I'm headed uptown, and you're headed downtown, I'm on my own for transportation home? Because that would be the most New York thing you could do right now."

"Or," I say, a breath catching in my chest. "It's the part of the date where I tell you I'm in love with you. Always have been, and always will be."

I promised myself I wouldn't say it, and that I'd continue to let her take the lead. The last thing I'd ever want to do is make Jenna uncomfortable.

"Well," Jenna laughs. "That wouldn't be very New York at all. But we didn't meet on a dating app, so perhaps, you and I clearly are not real New Yorkers."

Her eyes catch mine, and her mouth hangs open when she realizes I'm not trying to be funny. I am laying my heart on the line, and I can only imagine the fear my face conveys right now.

"Oh." She looks down. "We're doing this." Jenna shakes her head and looks at me. We stop talking as another horse and carriage go by us on the bridge.

"If you aren't in the same place, I want you to know it's okay. I had to tell you. You don't have to feel the same way or be ready. But I couldn't let more time pass without saying it." My voice trails off.

I've often wondered how to love someone best. I know what love shouldn't be—selfish and self-serving. I want to love someone the way I hope to be loved. And I've been thinking about this for a long time over the past few months. And first and foremost, I'd want to know someone loved me. And what they do with that is entirely up to them.

Jenna puts her hand up to her face.

"I'm not handling this well." Jenna pulls the sweater she's wearing of mine up to her chin. "But it's because I have a million thoughts and words flooding my brain simultaneously, and I want them to make sense when I say them."

"It's okay." I wrap my arms around myself when a gust of wind comes up. "I needed you to know. I don't expect anything from you."

"Robby." Jenna takes my arm. "I can't believe I left the way I did. Because yeah, I love you too. Always have. Always will."

"You do?" I take her hand in mine, allowing myself to feel hope in her words. "But you."

"There was so much up in the air at the end of the summer. I needed space from everything. I needed to process and didn't think I could do that with you in my life. But I wasn't here for long when I realized what I walked away from. I should have told you how I felt and asked you to be patient, but I couldn't ask you to wait until I sorted out my life. Or felt like I deserved you."

I take her elbow in my hand. "I would have waited."

She shakes her head. "I didn't feel like I could ask you to. I was so messed up after everything."

I wrap my arms around Jenna and hold her against me. "Loving each other is a really good first step."

She moves to her toes, wraps her arms around me, and kisses me. "A fancy restaurant and telling you love me. You set the bar really high for future dates."

I cup Jenna's face, and smile into our kiss.

We stand on the bridge and hold each other. There is so much lost time to make up for. I never want to be apart from her. "Is it too presumptuous to ask if you want to see my new place? I know it's our first date and all."

Jenna gets off of her toes and weaves her fingers into mine. "We've been doing this dance for two, long years, and I'm done. I'd love to see your place."

Epilogue

Jenna

I NEVER THOUGHT I'D BE THE girl who'd move to New York City and move in with a guy, but after my one-year lease was up on September first, I moved into Robby's place, and it's already been three months of living together. The finances of having two separate places made no sense. My place is cute, but I stay at Robby's flat every night. We contemplated finding an apartment together so it wouldn't be me moving in with him, but his place is perfect. Like, ridiculously perfect.

"Chinese or Thai tonight?" Robby hands me a glass of wine and sits on the couch next to me. I move my laptop to the table, grab his feet, and put them in my lap.

"Neither." I apply pressure to his arches, and he moans. "Didn't you get Liam's text? He wants us to meet him at Rockefeller Center to ice skate."

Robby raises an eyebrow. "You want to ice skate?"

"Yes, Robby, please." I move his legs off of me and throw my body on him. I place my chin on his chest, looking at him. "You know December is my favorite month in the city. We need to get out and do everything. Especially before we leave for Wheaton in a few days."

Robby sighs and then leans forward and kisses me. "You know I can't say no to you."

"Yay." I jump off Robby and run to our bedroom to put on some warmer clothes.

Robby is great at humoring me and letting me be a tourist, even though this is where we live now. If you haven't experienced New York this time of year, you haven't experienced romance and magic. Everything is lit up, white, and merry. Even the people who live in the city are nicer this time of year. And tomorrow is my last class at the Columbia School of Journalism, and I'll have my M.S. in Documentary Journalism, and then a day after that, we fly back to Minnesota for Christmas. We don't come back to the city until after New Year's, so when Liam reached out to us earlier to ask us to ice-skate, it's all I've thought about all day.

"What time's your class tomorrow?" Robby helps me get my arms through the sleeves.

"Not until eleven." I stick out my bottom lip and feign crying. "And then I'm done with school. It's so sad."

Robby laughs. "Think about how much money you'll have now that you aren't giving everything to Columbia."

"True," I agree.

Robby

WE WALK DOWN THE SIDEWALK as light, and fluffy snow begins to fall. Jenna looks up at the sky and holds her hands out.

"This is perfect." Jenna lets snowflakes land on her tongue.

Jenna has no idea, but I put Liam up to this entire ploy. He and some of the friends we've met living in the city are meeting us to ice-skate, and then I have a room reserved at a restaurant in the Rockefeller Center where some other friends are meeting us. There should be about twenty-five people in total. One of my hands holds Jenna's, and my other one pats my pocket to ensure the box is safe. It is.

This past year has been incredible. I knew I'd marry this girl when she told me she loved me back. I'm also practical, and I wanted Jenna to finish her degree and me to get more established with Teaching America and cohabitate.

Sometimes at night, when I can't sleep, I lie awake and think about how differently things could have gone. I always thought people didn't end up together because of some external conflict or unrequited feelings. Sometimes, we pass through life, and things don't work out because of unspoken truths and a lack of vulnerability to tell people exactly how we feel.

Jenna and I have talked a lot about this. The importance of timing in relationships and the importance of saying how we feel, even if we're worried the other person isn't in the same place. I always wanted to protect Jenna from everything, especially because of what she'd gone through, and I wasted time by not saying things.

I had assumptions about what she wanted or didn't want. She has shared where her head was at. And the entire time, since that first summer over two years ago, we loved each other but didn't want to lose the other person by telling them. When I thought that I may not have her in my life right now because I was scared of what her reaction would be. That thought scares the shit out of me.

"Look at the tree. It never loses its wonder." Jenna points to the giant tree at Rockefeller Center, with its bright golden lights, as it stretches high into the sky. "Can we stop there first?"

"Of course." I squeeze Jenna's hand as she practically runs toward the tree. My plan is going perfectly.

We reach the tree, and she stands there, staring at it in complete wonderment. I take the box out of my pocket, and I'm sure I will pass out from the nerves. I know she will say yes, but I've never done this before. I get down on one knee.

"Isn't it the most beautiful thing you've ever seen?" Jenna turns, and when she doesn't see me at eye level, she looks down.

She raises her eyebrows and puts her hands over her mouth. I only have eyes for Jenna now, but I can feel the energy of people around us, stopping to witness.

"Jenna." My voice is shaky, and a tear escapes my eye, and I flick it away. "It was a year ago that we first said our I love yous." Jenna nods her head. She's crying too.

"And knowing that you love me has made this the best year of my life. But I've loved you since we were kids, and I've been in love with you since the first moment you made fun of my clothes three years ago."

Jenna laughs, and I do too. I'm so off script at this point, and my nerves are causing my brain and thoughts to jumble, but it doesn't even matter.

I stand up. Shit. Am I supposed to stand? I haven't asked the question yet.

"Jenna Eleanor Abram, will you make me the happiest man in the world and allow me to be your husband?"

People around us clap and holler before Jenna even has a chance to answer. But then she yells yes, throws her arms around me, and I spin her. Shit, the ring. I take her glove off, place the ring on her finger, and pull her into a kiss.

We both have wet cheeks, and I'm not sure whose tears they are at this point.

"How about that ice skating?" Liam comes up from behind and puts his arms around us.

Jenna doesn't look away from her ring. "You knew?" She asks him, and Liam laughs.

We skate for a while, and I hold Jenna's left hand, the one with the ring. The ring I gave her. There are couples around us, happily gazing into each other's eyes or looking stressed and uncertain. We all have our story, and mine and Jenna's aren't more or less significant than anyone else's. Love is what sustains us. It helps us continue and motivates us to be better versions of ourselves.

We all have a love story. Sometimes the road is easy. And sometimes it's full of bumps, bruises, and regrets. I'll never take for granted that the most amazing person I've ever met loves me back. How many of us can say that?

Jenna puts her arm around me. "Damn, I'm happy."

THANK YOU FOR READING JENNA and Robby's story. If you enjoyed *Between Then and Now*, reviews are the best way to show love for the author.

Check out more from Leah at
https://bronzewoodbooks.com/leah-omar/

About the Author

WHEN SHE ISN'T WRITING NOVELS featuring strong female leads on a path to self-discovery, Leah Omar makes her career at a global medical device company. From Eyota, Minnesota, she holds bachelor's degrees in communications and English literature and a master's in business administration from Augsburg University in Minneapolis.

As a writer, Leah is devoted to giving her readers contemporary love stories that make us remember that we have more similarities than differences, and that love can conquer all. When Leah's not busy writing women's fiction and romance, she can be found watching a basketball game on TV, traveling somewhere far away, eating something spicy, or trying to shape the lives of her two amazing kids.

Leah now calls Minneapolis home, which she shares with her husband and two kids.

Check out more from Leah at
https://bronzewoodbooks.com/leah-omar/.

Made in the USA
Monee, IL
29 September 2023

43660327R00157